The Hardy Boys®
in
The Phantom Freighter

Other Hardy Boys ® Mystery Stories in Armada

* *For contractural reasons, Armada has been obliged to publish from No. 57 onwards before publishing Nos. 40–56. These missing numbers will be published as soon as possible.*

IMPRIMÉ EN FRANCE

The Hardy Boys ® Mystery Stories

The Phantom Freighter

Franklin W. Dixon

Armada

First published in the U.K. in 1977 by
William Collins Sons & Co. Ltd., London and Glasgow.
First published in Armada in 1985 by
Fontana Paperbacks,
8 Grafton Street, London W1X 3LA.

'The Hardy Boys' is a trademark of the Stratemeyer Syndicate,
registered in the United States Patent and Trademark Office.

Made and printed for
William Collins Sons & Co. Ltd, Glasgow

CONTENTS

With a startled cry Joe leapt back, but too late!

·1·

A Strange Substitute

"WHAT an odd letter!" exclaimed Frank Hardy, running a hand through his dark hair. "I wonder what the man wants."

His blond brother Joe, who was seventeen and a year younger, studied the sheet of paper. "Thaddeus McClintock," he said, reading the signature. "Never heard of him."

"Since he's living at the Bayport Hotel, he's probably a stranger in town. Who do you suppose told him about us?"

The boys were draped over upholstered chairs in the Hardys' living room. Their mother Laura, smiling at their relaxed teenage postures, said, "Any one of many people."

The letter, which had arrived in the morning mail, was addressed to Frank and Joe Hardy and read:

I have heard that you are young men with your feet on the ground and wonder if you would call and have a talk with me. I have an interesting job for you if you care to take it.

Frank looked at his brother. "What do you say?

9

There's no harm in talking to Mr McClintock."

"Please be careful," said Mrs Hardy. The slender, pretty woman went on, "The man may be a schemer of some kind. If he should ask any questions about your father, be on your guard."

"That," said Frank, "is Rule Number One in this household and we're not likely to forget it."

"Don't worry," Joe added in an assuring tone. "If this McClintock should try to pry, we don't know where Dad is, when he's expected, or what case he's working on." He grinned. "Come to think of it, we *don't* know. Do you, Mother?"

Mrs Hardy shook her head and chuckled. "No, I don't. But that's not unusual."

Fenton Hardy was a renowned private detective. Trained in the New York Police Department, he had left the big city to work entirely on his own, and with phenomenal success.

His sons had inherited their father's natural ability and had been carefully taught the most modern scientific detective methods.

Frank and Joe drove to the Bayport Hotel, and asked to see Mr McClintock. "Sorry," the clerk said. "He's not here right now. Went out about half an hour ago, but left a message for you. You're to come back this afternoon."

"Who is this Mr McClintock?" Frank asked. "Where does he come from? Is he young or old?"

The hotel clerk, who had been a friend of the Hardys for years, looked surprised. "You don't know him? Well, he's been living here for the past three months—is a little beyond middle age—doesn't say much."

"What's his line?" Joe asked.

"He doesn't work, but pays his bills promptly. Doesn't seem to have any friends here in Bayport. Maybe that's because he acts so secretive."

"Thanks," Frank said. "Guess that'll hold us until this afternoon."

He and Joe returned home, more interested than ever in meeting Mr McClintock. As they entered, they heard a woman talking excitedly.

"Aunt Gertrude!" said Joe. "And she's on the war-path!"

Aunt Gertrude- was Mr Hardy's unmarried sister, who had come to live with the family some time before. She was tall, peppery, and had an unpredictable temper. But beneath all the bluster she was a kindly soul who loved her nephews dearly.

"Laura, this box seems to be full of raw wool!" Aunt Gertrude was saying. "And *mine* contained valuable family papers. I'm going to call the express company and give them a piece of my mind!"

"What's wrong, Aunty?" Frank asked as he and Joe strolled in. "Have you been swindled?"

"Not swindled. No. Just—" She gasped in exaspera-tion. "I'm expecting a carton with some things I had left with a friend a few years ago. But they delivered the wrong one!" She pointed to the box lying on the floor. "I opened it without checking the label."

Joe looked at the box. "It's for a James Johnson," he stated. "One forty-two Springdale Avenue."

"That's right," Aunt Gertrude said. "Obviously the

shipping people delivered my carton to Mr Johnson and his to me. I'm going to call the express company and give them a piece of my mind."

"Take it easy, Aunty," Frank said. "Mistakes do happen."

Miss Hardy went to the telephone and dialled. As the conversation went on, Aunt Gertrude became more annoyed. "Now you listen to me!" she said, but the clerk at the other end insisted on doing all the talking. Finally Aunt Gertrude hung up. "They won't do a thing until tomorrow!" she complained. "Meanwhile, my carton may be opened by these Springdale Avenue people. And that," she added grimly, "must not happen!"

"How can you stop it?" asked Joe, a twinkle in his eyes.

"Very easily. You and Frank will have to go there and make the exchange. Right now!"

Frank looked at his watch. It was nearly time for lunch, and he and Joe wanted to call on Mr McClintock directly afterwards.

"No excuses," Miss Hardy said firmly. "It won't take you any time to drive out there. I'll whip up a strawberry shortcake while you're gone."

"In that case," Frank said, laughing, "we'll leave right away." He picked up the carton and went out the door. Joe followed.

A few minutes later they reached the east side of Bayport. Frank turned into Springdale Avenue. By the time they passed a small stone house numbered fifty-two, they had entered a section where the sidewalks came to an end and buildings were far apart. The car bumped along an uneven dirt road.

"We're practically out in the country," said Joe. "I'll bet we're beyond the city limits. Maybe there isn't any one hundred and forty-two at all!"

A short distance ahead and set quite far back from the road, they could see a large frame house, surrounded by a picket fence. A small barn stood behind it.

"This might be the place," Joe said as they neared it. Then he yelled excitedly, "Joe! Look! The barn's on fire!"

A curl of white smoke rolled out from an upper window. It was followed by a heavy black puff and a flicker of red flame.

Frank drove through the open gate and stopped in front of the house. Joe leaped out, ran up the steps, and hammered on the front door. There was no response. Joe tried the doorknob.

"Locked! No one at home!" he shouted. "Go get the fire engines, Frank!"

Frank swung the car around and roared back towards the road. Joe jumped off the porch and raced to the barn. By this time smoke was pouring from all the upper windows and flames were eating through the shingled roof.

Joe's first thought was for any animals that might be trapped inside. He tried to get in, but the doors were locked securely by a chain and padlock.

The boy ran around the building until he found a small side door, but this too was locked. Catching sight of a window, he rushed to it. A glance through the dusty glass revealed two stalls. They were empty.

Sheets of angry flame and billows of smoke now

leaped up from the floor of the barn. *And not far away stood a large cardboard carton!*

"That must be Aunt Gertrude's!" Joe thought. "I'll have to get it out!"

The window was so small Joe knew he could not crawl through it. He ran back to the side door and thrust his shoulder against the wood. The door creaked but did not give.

Looking around, he spotted a woodpile at the back of the house, with an axe beside the chopping block. He rushed across the yard, snatched up the axe, and dashed back to the barn.

·2·

The Three-Cornered Scar

JOE swung the axe. *Thud!* He swung again, but the wood was tough and the lock was stout.

Flames had broken through the roof in a dozen places now, and the upper part of the barn was a roaring inferno. Black smoke swirled towards Joe.

Suddenly he heard the sharp blast of a horn and the squeal of brakes. Frank was back. He leaped out of the convertible and ran towards his brother.

"Phoned the firemen from that house down the road," he called out. "But they won't get here in time to do any good. What are you up to?"

"Help me . . . break down . . . this door!" Joe gasped as he swung the axe again. "The lost carton is in there!"

Frank caught sight of a four-by-four propped against the side of the barn a few yards away. "Here's a battering ram! Better than the axe!"

Holding the wood firmly, they drove it against the door. At the very first impact the boards splintered. They drew back and rammed again. This time the lock snapped and the door fell in with a crash. Dense clouds of smoke poured through the opening.

As Joe looked into the burning building he knew he must act quickly to retrieve the valuable carton.

"Stand by," he said to Frank. "I'm going in."

"Watch yourself," warned Frank. "Stay close to the floor!"

Joe nodded. Taking a deep breath of fresh air, he held it in his lungs and crept across the barn towards the carton.

In a few seconds his groping fingers found it. He grabbed the twine and dragged the carton towards the door. But he felt as if his lungs would burst!

When Joe emerged, his eyebrows were singed, his skin parched. He drew in deep breaths of the fresh air and grinned weakly at his brother.

By this time help was arriving. Cars were driving into the yard. A siren wailed as a fire engine raced down Springdale Avenue. The barn, however, was doomed. The firemen turned their efforts to saving the house, which was threatened by flying sparks.

When the owner of the place and his wife drove into the yard half an hour later, their home was safe but nothing was left of the barn but a blackened foundation and a heap of smoking ashes. Learning that the Hardy boys had given the alarm, they came over to thank them.

"It was lucky you happened to be driving along and saw the smoke," the man said.

"We didn't just happen to come along," Frank told him. "As a matter of fact we were coming to make an exchange of cartons. We brought yours. The express company delivered ours here by mistake, and we rescued it from the barn, Mr Johnson."

"Johnson? My name's not Johnson. It's Phillips. No one named Johnson lives here."

The Hardys stared incredulously. Joe rushed to the carton addressed to Johnson and brought it over. He noticed now that there was no mention of the sender.

Mrs Phillips looked at it and shook her head. "I don't expect anything, and this obviously is not for us." She turned to Joe and pointed to the box he had taken from the barn. "Do you mean to say that you went into the burning barn after that? There's nothing in it but old newspapers. I was waiting for the junkman to pick them up!"

Frank and Joe were flabbergasted. To think Joe had taken such a risk for a lot of old newspapers!

Just then an express-company truck drove into the yard. The driver got out and came over to them. He knew the Hardys.

"Your aunt called up the office a while ago about a carton," he said to Frank. "So I thought I'd better drive out and check up on it. I delivered one to your house and one to this place. Fellow by the name of Johnson signed for it. Maybe—"

"What!" Mr Phillips interrupted. "My wife and I have been away several days and the house was locked up!"

"Maybe so," returned the driver. "But I delivered a box here this morning just the same. There was a man standing on the porch when I got here. He signed for it." The driver took out his book and flipped through the pages. "Here's the name."

The boys studied the scrawled signature of James Johnson.

"Something's strange about this," Frank said. "Do you mind if I copy the signature?" Using a piece of plain paper and a carbon from the back of the driver's book he made a tracing.

"What did the man look like?" Joe asked.

"He was about forty, beady-eyed, with a low forehead. Had a scar high up on his right cheek. A three-cornered scar, like a triangle."

Mr Phillips looked grim. "I'd like to meet this guy and find out what he was doing here. I'll bet he set my barn on fire!"

Joe spoke up. "If Johnson got the wrong carton, maybe he'll go to the express office to pick up the right one. Suppose we ask the police to question him if he does?"

"Good idea," Phillips agreed.

"Well, I don't want any more trouble," said the driver. "There's enough already." Turning to the Hardys, he added, "I'll take this carton along."

As Frank and Joe drove back to Bayport, they discussed the mysterious affair of the two boxes. What had happened to Aunt Gertrude's? Had the man with the scar taken it away? Or had it been destroyed in the fire? In any case, Frank thought, the man probably had not given his real name, and would not show up at the express office to claim his property.

"I wonder how Aunt Gertrude will take the news," Joe said glumly.

"I hate to tell her," said Frank. "She made it plain that she didn't want anyone to see the contents of the carton."

As they passed through the downtown section of Bayport, Joe suggested that since it was past lunchtime they have a quick bite to eat and then call on Mr

McClintock. Frank telephoned home, asking that the strawberry shortcake be saved until later, but refrained from mentioning the carton.

"I'm glad you called," Mrs Hardy said. "I have a chore for you." She asked if the boys would stop at a haberdashery and buy socks and handkerchiefs for their father.

"Okay, Mother," Frank promised.

When they entered the Bayport Hotel half an hour later, Joe said, "I hope Mr McClintock is back."

The clerk nodded as they approached the desk. "Just in time," he said. "Your man returned a while ago. He's waiting for you. Room 201."

McClintock was slightly stoop-shouldered. He had sharp, fidgety eyes and a nervous habit of snapping his fingers when he talked. He greeted the boys affably and asked them to sit down.

"I've heard interesting things about you Hardys," he said. "Now I'll come right to the point. My doctor has advised me that I need a complete change in my way of living. Says I brood too much."

With that the man bounded from his chair and started pacing back and forth. His face was grim. Then he stopped and continued bitterly, "The doctor would brood, too, if his lifework had been completely— Well, that's beside the point. Anyway, here's my proposition:

"I want to go on a trip. A long trip. And I'd like you to go with me. You must plan it and make all the arrangements."

After a moment of astonished silence, Joe gasped, "You—want—us to go?"

"Exactly. You're what the doctor ordered. Young

people. To cheer me up. After I see how clever you are at planning the trip, I may even give you a mystery to solve."

Frank and Joe glanced at each other. Was this man a nut? Did McClintock really have a mystery to solve? Or was he just trying to interest the boys in going with him?

"Where do you want to travel?" Frank asked.

"How should I know?" rasped McClintock. "That's up to you."

"But you say you want to go on a long trip . . ."

"Exactly. And I don't care where. I just want to get away. And I want company. And not be troubled with making arrangements."

"But what kind of vacation do you like best, sir?" Joe enquired. "A motor trip, a hike, a sea voyage? Do you think your health could stand a long tour?"

"Do I look *that* sick?" McClintock demanded. He glanced narrowly at the two boys. "You seem mighty doubtful about it. Don't make up your minds right away. Go home and talk it over. Maybe you think I'm crazy and you don't want to have anything to do with me.

"Well, I'm not crazy and I'm not really sick," he went on. "Just need a change. After you mull it over, maybe you'll decide to accept my proposition. I'll pay all the expenses, and when the trip is over, you'll be paid. Money, if you like. Or something else."

"For example?" Frank said.

Mr McClintock shook his head. "I'm not saying. But I'm a man of my word and I guarantee you won't be disappointed."

The boys did not know what to make of the extraordinary offer. They were convinced that the man was perfectly sane, although undoubtedly eccentric.

"We'll be glad to think it over," said Frank. "It isn't the sort of thing we can decide right off. Not quite our line, you know."

"I told you you'd be paid," McClintock replied shrewdly. "You name a figure. If it's too high, I'll say so. If it's too low, I won't open my mouth."

"It's not the money," Joe objected. "As a matter of fact, we'd probably be more interested in—"

"Hah! The other reward!" McClintock interrupted. "I promise you! It's more valuable than money!"

· 3 ·

Suspicion

"IT won't be easy to make plans unless we know how you want to travel," said Joe. "How about a motor trip?"

McClintock scowled and shook his head. "I said that I'd leave the arrangements to you. But I should have told you I don't like cars. A motor trip is out."

"A train trip, then?" Frank suggested.

McClintock wrinkled his nose. "I can't sleep on trains."

"How about a plane? Maybe a visit to Europe?" Joe ventured.

"They go too fast. Get over there too soon. I want a long trip."

"Ocean liner?" Frank said.

"No sir! Too many people. I'd have to dress up. Too fancy. That's not the sort of thing I mean at all."

The boys sighed. Mr McClintock certainly was hard to please!

"Fact of the matter is," he went on, "I know what kind of trip I *don't* like. But I don't know what I *do* like. That's your job. Figure something out."

Frank and Joe got up to leave. "We'll think about it," said Frank. "As soon as we've decided, we'll let you know."

As they left the hotel, Frank said, "For a guy who just wants a vacation and doesn't care where he goes, he seems mighty particular. I'm stumped."

"We forgot a bicycle tour," Joe quipped. He added quickly, "Look! Here comes Chet!"

Down the street trudged their friend, round-faced, stocky Chet Morton. He lived on a farm outside of Bayport. Usually Chet was the picture of irresponsible bliss, but today his brows were knit in a frown, and when he greeted the Hardys his voice sounded gloomy.

"Hi," he mumbled.

"Going fishing?" Joe asked, indicating a case Chet was carrying under his arm.

"No," he replied. "But maybe you'd like to. I'll sell this rod cheap. Genuine bamboo. I bought it for my father."

"Didn't he like it?"

Chet shook his head. "It was on sale, too. Forty-five dollars."

Frank whistled. "How did you ever save that much money?"

"To tell the truth, I didn't. I borrowed it from the money Dad gave me to buy some seed. I was sure he wouldn't mind, because the rod was a real bargain. Now I've got to earn forty-five dollars to pay him back."

"Use the rod to catch fish, then sell the fish," suggested Joe.

Chet looked at him sourly. "Forty-five dollars' worth of fish? You've got to be kidding. I may be able to make some money selling flies, though."

"Flies? Who'd want flies?" asked Frank.

"I don't mean houseflies. Artificial ones, for fishing. I sent away for a book that tells how to tie them. Want to come to my house and help me?"

The Hardys recognized this as one more of Chet's schemes, usually impractical, for making money. He was always embarking on some kind of venture. Every time Frank and Joe agreed to help him they found themselves doing most of the work.

"Too busy to tie flies," Frank replied promptly. "A man just made us a proposition and we have to do some thinking about it." He told Chet about their interview with Mr McClintock.

Chet listened with interest. "Boy, he even hinted at a mystery! What do you suppose it is?"

"Haven't the faintest idea," Joe said.

"Right now he seems less worried about solving the mystery than going on a vacation," Frank added.

"Why not suggest a fishing trip?" Chet said. "I'll bet he'd go for that. No trains, no planes, no cars, no ocean liners. Just a nice lazy fishing trip."

"Sounds like a pretty fair idea," Joe remarked. "He might like it."

"Good!" Chet exclaimed. "You can sell him this fishing rod. After all, he'll need equipment."

But the Hardys were not to be lured into Chet's little sales scheme that easily.

"We'll think about it," Frank promised. "If McClintock wants to go on a fishing trip and if he really needs equipment and if he wants to pay forty-five dollars for a rod and if your rod is worth that much—we'll ask him to talk to you."

"Humph—a lot of ifs," Chet grumbled. "I'll probably have the rod sold to someone else by then." He sauntered off. "See you later."

Frank and Joe were about to get into their car and drive home when Frank remembered his mother's shopping request. There was a haberdashery near the hotel, and the boys went inside.

A customer was standing at the counter when they entered. He was a hulk of a man about forty, with beady eyes and a low forehead. But the most significant detail, the boys noticed, was a scar high on his right cheek.

The man, after glancing at them, turned back to the counter and examined some belts the sales assistant had brought out. Frank and Joe retreated to the back of the store for a whispered conference.

"Frank, do you think he's that Johnson fellow?"

"Sure answers the description. I'll phone the expressman to come over and identify this guy. If he leaves, follow him!"

Frank went to a phone booth at the corner. Joe pretended to be examining a rack of sports jackets. The customer was in no hurry. He purchased a belt, then looked at neckties. He was about to buy one when Frank returned.

"Expressman hasn't returned from his route," he told his brother quietly. Then he walked up to the counter to get a better look at the man's face. Noticing some neckties the suspect had discarded, Frank asked pleasantly, "Have you finished with these?"

"Yeah."

The boy looked directly into the stranger's face. The scar was triangular in shape!

The man noticed that Frank was staring. Frank

quickly averted his eyes, but the man glared angrily at him, picked up his change, and thrusting the purchase into his pocket, strode out.

"That'll teach you to mind your manners," the assistant said with a chuckle. "Say, where're you going? I thought you wanted to buy something!"

Frank and Joe were already at the door. "We'll be back," Frank called.

By this time the man was nearly half a block away, walking rapidly. Frank and Joe jumped into their car and followed. He turned right at the end of the block.

"He's going towards the harbour," said Joe.

"So are we!" Frank swung into the street leading to the waterfront. The boys caught sight of the scarred man again. He glanced back over his shoulder.

"Hope he doesn't recognize us," Frank said, "or he'll know he's being tailed."

The fellow quickened his pace. Then quickly he stepped into an alley that opened between two buildings and broke into a run.

Frank swung the car into the alley, but found it blocked by a truck unloading supplies. The man dodged around the front of it.

"I'll get out and meet you at the other end," said Joe. He jumped out of the convertible and ran after the suspect.

Frank swiftly backed out into the street again and drove around the block. When he reached the far end of the alley, Joe was waiting, but the suspect was not in sight.

"Gave me the slip," Joe muttered in exasperation.

"I'll bet he's Johnson all right. Otherwise why did he run?"

"We might catch sight of him around the docks," Frank suggested. "He was heading that way."

"It's worth trying," agreed Joe and hopped into the car.

They rode down the hill to Bayport's waterfront district. Frank parked the car and they began their search on foot. But there was no sign of the man with the scar.

"Guess we'll have to give up," Frank said finally. "We'll come back later."

As the boys walked through a large pier shed they stopped to watch the busy scene. Tons of supplies were being loaded on to a waiting freighter.

Frank snapped his fingers in excitement. "Hey, Joe, I have an idea!"

"What is it?"

"About Mr McClintock's trip. Why not a voyage by freighter?"

"He said he didn't want to take a sea voyage," Joe reminded him.

"He didn't want to go on a passenger liner because of the crowds and he'd have to dress up," said Frank. "A freighter's different, though."

"You might have something." Joe glanced at the big ship. "And I wouldn't mind a trip like that myself."

On the way home they discussed their new idea excitedly. It seemed like the perfect solution to Mr McClintock's problem.

Frank parked in front of the haberdashery again and Joe went in to purchase the socks and handkerchiefs for his father. He asked the assistant if he knew the scar-faced customer. The salesman answered "No," but from what little the man had said, he had gathered that he was a seaman.

When the boys reached home Mrs Hardy greeted them at the door with the welcome news that their father had just returned. Aunt Gertrude wanted to know what happened to her missing carton. When told about the fire, she became very upset.

"The express company ought to be sued!" she declared. "The idea of handing over my box to a total stranger. It probably was destroyed in the fire!"

"I'm sure the express company will do what it can, Aunty," Frank said.

Miss Hardy replied that money could not repay her for her family papers and personal letters contained in the lost carton. Mr Hardy came out of his study and wanted to know why his sister was so excited. The boys told him about the expressman's mistake and their adventure in the blazing barn.

"There's something fishy about the whole affair," Fenton Hardy said thoughtfully. "Gertrude, why don't you talk to an official of the express company and ask him to check further."

"I certainly will," she replied.

That evening at dinner the detective related stories of his travels in connection with his work during the past two weeks. Most of his time had been spent with specialists dealing in rare documents and valuable autographs whose businesses were seriously threatened by skilful forgeries that had appeared on the market.

The fakes were so clever that even experts had been fooled by them.

"The forgers also compose letters on aged paper," Mr Hardy said. "That's how I got my first clue."

"Tell us about it, Dad," Joe said.

The forgers, his father explained, were not well-versed in old phraseology, and that was how their swindles had been discovered. But they were skilled counterfeiters and evidently had the help of a clever chemist in "ageing" the paper. Mr Hardy had visited half a dozen large cities in his efforts to run down the gang, but so far had met with little success.

While the family was eating Aunt Gertrude's delectable strawberry shortcake, Frank brought up the subject of Mr McClintock's trip.

After hearing how eccentric the man was, Aunt Gertrude predicted trouble for her nephews. "No telling what a person like that might do," she said firmly. "Leave you stranded in some foreign country, or never pay you a cent for all your trouble."

Mrs Hardy also voiced concern. "Fenton, I think you should look into this," she suggested.

It was decided that Mr Hardy would accompany his sons to the hotel and speak to Mr McClintock. With his expert insight, he might be able to settle the matter quickly.

The next morning, after talking with Mr McClintock for nearly an hour, Mr Hardy gave consent to the trip.

"I must go now," he said. "I'll leave you three to make plans and trust you'll work out something enjoyable."

After he had left, Mr McClintock turned to the boys.

"Okay. If you can only figure out how and where to travel . . ."

"We have a suggestion, sir," Joe said. "How about a voyage by ocean freighter?"

The man scowled. "Ocean freighter? You mean an old tramp steamer? Ridiculous. Dirty. Smelly. Poor food."

"It wouldn't be that bad," Frank spoke up quickly. "A modern freighter is a very clean ship. Some of them make a business of carrying a few passengers. We'd pick one of those and see that the food and accommodations were A-okay."

"You'd find it a lot of fun," put in Joe. "They go to unusual places."

"Well, look into it. If you discover the right kind of ship, let me know."

As the boys left the hotel Frank advised that they try to locate a freighter that carried passengers.

"We'd better get it settled before Mr McClintock has time to change his mind," he said, laughing.

"Right!" agreed Joe. "He's such a strange guy you can't tell what he'll do or say next. I like him, though. By the way, Frank, did you notice he steered clear of mentioning anything about the mystery?"

"Yes, I did. Guess it was only a lure, after all."

The boys rode to the docks, looking for the freighter that they had seen the day before. It had already sailed, but another ship was in its berth. Frank spoke to a longshoreman coming from the loading shed.

"Do you know where we can find a freighter that carries passengers?"

The man gestured with a grimy thumb. "Try the

Hawk. She's loading now."

Frank and Joe climbed up a ladder running from the dockside to the ship's rail high above. A sandy-haired seaman in a sweater and dungarees emerged from the galley and glanced at them curiously.

"We're looking for the captain," Frank explained.

"He's up forward. What do you want him for?"

"We'd like to ship as passengers."

"Nothing doing. We don't carry passengers."

"But we were told—"

"You heard me. No passengers."

"I think we'll see the captain, anyway," Frank said and the boys turned away. They walked down the narrow space between the rail and the open hatches towards the officers' quarters.

"Hey! Stay away from the captain!" the seaman bellowed.

"I wonder what's eating him," Joe said.

"Probably just a grouch. Got up on the wrong side of the bunk this morning."

They passed by the gap of an open hatch. Then their way was barred by stacks of freight. Retracing their steps, Frank and Joe decided to go around the deckhouse. A huge net filled with boxes of cargo swung over from the dock towards the hatch.

"Have to watch your way around here," said Joe as a heavy steel boom swung in front of him. But Frank at that moment had turned to look for the unfriendly seaman.

"Duck!" Joe yelled.

· 4 ·

No Passengers

Frank did not dodge in time. The heavy boom struck him, carried the startled boy upwards, and swept him overboard!

Joe leaped to the railing. He saw Frank hurtle down past the steel side of the freighter, not three feet from the pier. His body, twisting and turning limply, hit the water with a resounding smack.

Instantly Joe scrambled on to the rail, balanced a moment, then dived.

It was nearly a thirty-foot drop, but he struck the water cleanly just a few yards from the place where Frank had disappeared. Under water, Joe opened his eyes. Catching sight of a dark object, he swam towards it, then shot to the surface, one arm around his unconscious brother.

Joe towed him towards a ladder hanging from the pier, wondering how badly Frank was hurt. He was greatly relieved when his brother made a convulsive movement and began to struggle and thrash about.

"It's okay. Take it easy," Joe muttered.

Two longshoremen, having seen Frank's mishap, had rushed to the edge of the dock. They reached down and hoisted the two boys out of the murky water. The men carried Frank to a small office inside the loading shed. Joe followed, breathless and frightened.

"Get a doctor!" the taller of the two longshoremen called out.

But the other acted instantly and started giving Frank first aid. Presently the•boy opened his eyes and looked around dully.

"Thank goodness you came to," said Joe.

"He wouldn't have if it hadn't been for you," said the tall longshoreman. "I saw the whole thing. He'd have drowned if you hadn't pulled him out."

Frank weakly smiled his thanks. "We'd better . . . go . . . home," he murmured.

He was carried to the convertible and Joe took the wheel. The men offered to go along, but Joe declined their assistance, saying he was sure that his brother would be all right.

At the Hardy house there was great consternation when the boys' mother and Aunt Gertrude saw Joe helping Frank up the stairs. They scurried about, talking, advising, and getting Frank to bed as fast as possible.

"I'm okay now," he insisted. "Just got a whale of a headache. That's all."

When the two women finally left the room, he said to Joe, who had showered and changed his clothes, "Listen. I think I was struck on purpose by that boom."

"Really?"

"Yes. I saw that guy who tried to get us off the *Hawk* motioning to someone on the dock. I'll bet he was signalling for him to swing the boom so it would hit us. But he won't get away with it!"

"You bet he won't!" Joe said grimly. He started downstairs.

"Don't go alone!" Frank called after him.

Before Joe had time to think about it, the front doorbell rang and he answered. Biff Hooper, a schoolmate and good friend of the Hardys, walked in. He was a blond six-footer and had muscles like steel.

"Hi!" Joe called. "You're just the guy I'm looking for. I need a bodyguard. Want to give a big tough guy a good punch?"

"Since when have you stopped doing that yourself?" Biff grinned as the two boys went out the door. On the way to the dock Joe explained what had happened.

Although he had superior strength, Biff Hooper never picked fights, and by the time they had reached the *Hawk* he had almost convinced Joe that the whole affair might have been an unavoidable accident. "There's no point in starting trouble," Biff advised.

"Just the same, I'm going aboard," declared Joe, "and finish what I started to do, namely see the captain."

The two mounted the ladder. This time no loading was going on. The sailor the Hardys had encountered before was not in sight. Two of the crew lounged on deck, and one man rose as the boys approached.

"What do you want?" he asked.

"To see your captain," Joe replied.

"What about?"

"I'll talk to him."

"You will, eh? Not if you don't find him. And I say you won't."

"Don't bully me!" Joe said fiercely and Biff cocked

his right fist in anticipation. A fight might have started if the captain himself had not appeared. Skipper Sharp lived up to his name. He was a tall, narrow-jawed, thin-featured man with piercing eyes.

"What's the matter?" he boomed, striding forward.

"I'm trying to book passage on a freighter for three people," Joe explained.

"You're on the wrong ship. Can't accommodate you," the captain replied shortly.

"You don't carry passengers?"

"We used to. But not any more. It didn't work out. There's no point in discussing it."

"We're willing to pay well—" Joe's attempt to continue the conversation was cut off.

"No passengers at any price. Get lost!"

Disappointed, Joe started down the ship's ladder. Biff followed.

As they left the dock, Biff expressed his indignation at their rude reception. "I don't see why the captain had to act like a jerk," he said. "You'd think we were a couple of criminals." Then he brightened. "Say, Joe, I know where you can book passsage!"

"Where?"

"At Klack's Agency. It's not far from here. Next block."

He led the way to a dingy-looking establishment with several blackboards in the window. On them were chalked such legends as *Cook Wanted, Fireman (First Class) for S.A., Cruise and Stokers Wanted.*

"A lot of freighter crews are signed up here," Biff explained. "I've heard they book passengers as a sideline."

Mr Klack was out. But a stringy-haired blonde girl inquired languidly what the boys wanted.

"Can you fix me up with freighter passage for three?" Joe asked.

The girl shook her head. "There are no ships in port —none takin' passengers, that is. Give me the names, and if somethin' turns up, I'll let you know."

Joe wrote down their names and addresses and thanked the girl. Joe drove Biff home, then returned to the Hardy house.

Aunt Gertrude had gone to the express office to press her complaint, and Frank had fallen asleep. Joe was telling his mother about the second visit to the *Hawk* when the telephone rang. It was Aunt Gertrude.

"Joe!" she called loudly. "Come down here right away. Quick!"

"But where are you, Aunty?"

"Why, at the express office, of course! There's a chance to solve the mystery. Hurry!"

"I'll be right down," Joe promised. He hung up and turned to his mother. "Aunty's on to something big. See you later."

Seconds later, he was on his way. When he drove up in front of the express company, Aunt Gertrude ran out, pointing to a truck about to pull away from the kerb. It was loaded with trunks, bags and boxes.

"Follow him, Joe!" Miss Hardy commanded, jumping into the car beside her nephew and slamming the door shut.

"Why? What's the rush?"

"You want to find out what's going on, don't you?"

"Sure."

"Then get going."

Joe accelerated as his aunt snapped the safety-belt buckle. "You mean the delivery man is going to lead us to your missing carton?" he asked.

Miss Hardy snorted, then assumed an attitude of patient tolerance. "No. There's no word about *my* carton. Now keep following him."

"Look, I'm sort of confused," Joe said, being careful not to tailgate the truck. "What's this all about?"

After giving Joe a few pointers on road safety, Aunt Gertrude said, "This morning a box that looks like mine and also like that other one with the raw wool arrived at the express office."

"Oh," said Joe. "And it's being delivered somewhere. You think that maybe James Johnson will be there to receive it?"

"Your brain's working now," Aunt Gertrude said. "The carton's marked for a Mrs Harrison. The truck's going there after making a few other deliveries. So I thought it wouldn't hurt to investigate."

"Good idea," Joe agreed. "By the way, Johnson never called for his carton, did he?"

"I forgot to ask."

The delivery man was the same one who had made the initial mistake. Joe was eager to reach the Harrison place, but the driver seemed to be in no hurry.

He delivered big parcels and little parcels, large boxes and small boxes to various parts of town. Finally, with only the carton left, he headed for the outskirts of Bayport. Joe followed doggedly.

At length the truck came to a stop in front of a handsome, modern home on a street with scattered houses. The driver unloaded the carton and carried it to the front steps.

"Now go see, Joe. Hurry!" his aunt urged.

Joe was out of the car and at the heels of the man as he rang the bell.

A grey-haired woman opened the door and looked sharply at them.

"Mrs Harrison?" asked the driver, setting the carton in the hall.

"Yes."

"Sign here, please," he said, handing her a pencil and pointing out a blank space on his pad.

Joe half expected the signature to be in the same handwriting as that of Johnson and the signer to be masquerading as a woman. But he was wrong. The woman's writing seemed definitely feminine, as was her voice.

"Is Mr Harrison home?" Joe inquired.

"*Mr* Harrison? Why—er—no," she replied haltingly.

"This is his carton, isn't it?" Joe went on, still clinging to a hope that his errand was not in vain.

"What is this?" Mrs Harrison snapped. "A teenage quiz programme?" She slammed the door.

The driver grinned. "Fool's errand for you, eh?" he said to Joe as they returned to the street.

"I'm afraid so," Joe replied ruefully and got back into the convertible.

When she heard the story Aunt Gertrude was convinced that the transaction was not entirely above board. "Ladies don't slam doors in people's faces," she said, annoyed. "Those who do are afraid of something."

Aunt Gertrude was so chagrined that she avoided mentioning the incident that evening. But the next morning she brought up the subject again and expressed her view about Mrs Harrison's conduct. "I never saw such bad manners," she exploded.

"Which Mrs Harrison is this?" asked Mrs Hardy.

"Oh, she lives on Mount Pleasant Drive," replied Aunt Gertrude. "Mrs Robert Harrison. A very rude woman."

"Why, Gertrude!" Mrs Hardy exclaimed, shocked. "I know Martha Harrison. She's a lovely person. You mustn't say such things about her."

"You may think she's a lovely person, Laura, but judging from her actions yesterday—"

"Yesterday?" Mrs Hardy repeated. "But Martha Harrison is out of town!"

· 5 ·

More Disappointment

"ARE you sure?" Joe asked his mother excitedly.

"Yes. Mrs Harrison is attending a convention of women's clubs in Highburg. There's no one home now because her husband is in Mexico."

Joe dashed to the telephone and called the Harrison number. There was no answer.

"I'm going there!" he declared. "Frank, feel well enough to come?"

"Sure do."

Mrs Hardy's revelation had convinced Joe that there might well be something strange about the delivery of the box after all.

They drove over to Mount Pleasant Drive. Frank rang the bell. No answer. A boy who was riding a bicycle along the street said he was a neighbour, and volunteered the information that the Harrisons had closed their house a week before and would not be back until the end of the month.

Frank and Joe returned home.

"I knew it!" declared Aunt Gertrude. "I knew there was something suspicious about that woman the moment I heard she slammed the door in your face, Joe."

"But why would she be living in the Harrison house?" Mrs Hardy asked, puzzled.

"I have a theory about that," Fenton Hardy said. "Sometimes burglars watch the social columns of the newspapers for names of people who are to be away. They learn when a house will be unoccupied, then rob it."

"Do you think there were thieves in the Harrison home?" Mrs Hardy cried.

The detective shrugged. "Perhaps. But not ordinary thieves. I suspect that some gang was using the Harrisons' home as a convenient address."

"For the delivery of cartons?" asked Frank.

"Exactly. And they probably contain stolen goods. The gang may be moving valuable stuff from state to state, and by using other people's names and addresses, they practically eliminate the risk of being traced."

"What a racket!" Joe exclaimed.

"It's not new. But it works," Mr Hardy said. "I suggest that you boys notify the express company. No doubt they'll turn the matter over to the police."

Now thoroughly engrossed in the case, Aunt Gertrude spoke up. "The carton that came here had raw wool in it, Fenton. That's not worth stealing, is it?"

The famous detective smiled at his sister. "No, of course not. But something valuable might have been hidden in the wool."

"Like what?"

"We'll have to wait and see," Mr Hardy replied, looking directly at his sons.

In the meantime Mrs Hardy had put in a long-distance call to Mrs Harrison, who was shocked at the news. She had given no one permission to use her house and would return immediately to see if anything had been stolen.

The boys drove downtown once again and called at the express office. The manager, Mr Nixon, was concerned and upset to hear that his firm's services were probably being used to move stolen goods.

"No one has claimed that carton addressed to Johnson," he said. "I'm going to open it, and if you're right, I'll certainly tell Police Chief Collig about it. Come along."

He led the way to a rear room. There was no carton in sight. All three searched the place, but in vain.

"Funny," said Mr Nixon, scratching his head. "It couldn't have walked away!"

"I'm afraid it has been stolen," said Frank. "That man Johnson was taking no chances."

"You'll report it to the police?" Joe suggested.

The manager shook his head. "I'd rather not do that just now. There would be damaging publicity. How about you two taking the case? I've heard a good deal about your success as detectives."

Frank and Joe hesitated. They did not know how they could accept in view of the trip with Mr McClintock. Frank explained this to the manager.

"Fair enough," Nixon replied. "But why not work on it until you leave on your trip? If it hasn't been cleared up by the time you go, I'll turn it over to the police."

"All right," said Frank. "We'll do what we can."

When the Hardys came out of the express office building, they were surprised to see Mr McClintock.

"Your aunt told me you were here," he explained. "I've been thinking about that freighter proposition you suggested. Doesn't sound too bad. But I don't know a thing about freighters. Do you suppose I could see one?"

"There's one in port now," said Frank. "It's called the *Hawk*. We can't book passage on it, but at least you'll see what a big freighter is like."

Mr McClintock climbed into the car. When they reached the waterfront, the *Hawk* was much lower in the water, though not loaded to capacity yet. A large sign said, *Positively No Visitors*. It was easy, however, to study the details of the ship from the dockside.

Mr McClintock was pleasantly surprised. "Might be all right to travel on a ship like that," he agreed. "I'll let you know."

"Why not come up to our house to dinner tonight?" Joe said. "We'll have more information by then. I left our names at an agency."

"Never eat much at night," said Mr McClintock. "Don't go out to dinner at people's houses because they always expect me to sit around for a couple of hours afterwards and it keeps me up long past my bed-time. Now if you want to make that lunch—"

"Lunch it is." Frank laughed. "Let me call the house and tell Mother you're coming."

Mr McClintock apparently enjoyed himself immensely at the meal. To the amazement of the boys, he and Aunt Gertrude took an immediate liking to each other. They chatted gaily about times past and present, even voicing approval of at least part of the new generation.

"Of course, my two nephews are unusual," Aunt Gertrude remarked.

"Quite so," Mr McClintock agreed.

The two shook hands warmly when their guest departed, and early that evening Mr McClintock telephoned, to say that he had made up his mind. He wanted to leave on a freighter trip right away. In fact, he had already picked his ship.

"The one we saw at the dock looks all right to me. Book passage on it at once and we'll sail as soon as it's ready."

Vainly Frank tried to explain that the *Hawk*'s captain had already refused them passage.

"Try them again. Offer double fare. That'll bring him around. I want to go on that boat!"

To please him, Frank telephoned Klack's Agency. Klack himself answered the call.

"No passengers," he said. "You couldn't go on the *Hawk* now anyway. She sailed a few minutes ago."

That, apparently, settled it. But the Hardy boys had not reckoned with a very persistent streak in Mr McClintock.

"I want to take a trip on that boat and I'm going to," he announced when Frank reported to him over the telephone.

"But how?" Frank asked. "She's gone!"

"We can find a fast motorboat and catch her," came the reply. "Don't you know where to get one?"

"We own a motorboat," Frank said. "It can go a good deal faster than a freighter and we might overtake the *Hawk* all right, but—"

"Then what are we waiting for? Throw some clothes

in a suitcase. I'll call for you in a taxi in ten minutes."

"But we'll have to find somebody to bring our boat back," Frank protested.

"That's your business," replied their client and hung up.

Mrs Hardy and Aunt Gertrude helped the boys pack, while Joe telephoned to several of their friends. Finally he reached Tony Prito, who was willing to go along and bring back their boat, the *Sleuth*, if the Hardys could get on the *Hawk*.

Mr McClintock was at the Hardy house on time, and ten minutes later the *Sleuth* was nosing its way out of the boathouse and roaring off into the twilight.

"When this Captain Sharp sees we're determined to go with him, he'll change his mind," predicted Mr McClintock.

Even though the *Hawk* had a good start, the Hardys knew that their boat would be able to overtake the freighter. The regular steamer channel was clearly marked by buoys, and as the *Sleuth* ate up the miles Frank and Joe were confident it would be only a matter of minutes before they would see the lights of the big ship ahead.

But they sped on and on, peering into the gloom.

"Thought you said this boat of yours was a speedy one," gibed McClintock. "Can't you catch up to a slow steamer?"

"There isn't a faster motorboat on Barmet Bay," spoke up Tony, quick to defend his friends' craft.

The moon rose, flooding the water with light. They could see to the mouth of the bay. The *Hawk* was not in sight.

"She's faster than I thought," said Frank. He put his boat to the limit of her power and they came out into the open sea. Nothing but water. No moving lights indicated the presence of any ship.

Frank swung the wheel. The *Sleuth* turned.

"Giving up?" demanded McClintock.

"Not entirely," Frank replied. "We'll go back to Bayport and find out the *Hawk*'s first port of call. If it's not far away, we can go there by car and board the ship."

McClintock grumbled a little, but he realized that there was no point in continuing the chase by sea. The *Sleuth* roared back to port. There the boys learned by phoning Klack at his home that the *Hawk* was to stop at Southport.

They took Mr McClintock to his hotel, then drove home. Before they went to bed, Frank telephoned the harbour master in Southport. The reply to his question left him astonished and bewildered.

"That freighter hasn't docked here," the harbour master said. "We aren't even expecting her!"

· 6 ·

The Morton Special

WHEN Frank and Joe reported to Mr McClintock the next morning that the *Hawk* had vanished mysteriously, he went into a tirade. But by this time the boys had become used to his outbursts and scarcely heard him.

Instead, their thoughts turned to the strange happenings in connection with the ship. The threatening seaman, the swinging boom that had knocked Frank into the water, the unpleasant captain, and now a new route for the *Hawk*, evidently determined upon in a hurry.

"—so do something. And do it quick!" Mr McClintock was saying. "I thought you were boys who got things done in a hurry!"

Frank gulped. "Sorry. Well, we'll find another freighter."

"I'll go and ask at Klack's," Joe offered. He hastened to the agency's office and told the man behind the counter about being on a waiting list for freighter passage for three. "What are the chances of getting passage?" Joe asked.

"Practically none at all."

"What do you mean?"

"Not many ships take passengers, and most of 'em are booked up."

"When can I see Mr Klack?"

"I'm Mr Klack."

"Oh," said Joe. "Thanks for the information last night."

"Glad to help you."

"Well, you have our phone number," Joe went on. "Please let us know when you get reservations. The sooner the better."

He returned to the hotel and reported the situation to Mr McClintock and Frank. As usual, McClintock fussed like a baby without a pacifier until Joe motioned his brother aside.

"Frank, I don't like that man Klack. I have a feeling he wouldn't give us reservations if he had any."

"But why?"

Joe shrugged. "I'm going to make an investigation of my own. Stay here a few minutes to soothe our client. I'll meet you at home."

Joe headed directly for the docks. A freighter which had come in at seven o'clock, he learned, usually carried six passengers. Hurrying to the captain, he asked if the Hardy party might take the outgoing trip.

"Sorry, son—" smiled the pleasant man—"but all space was reserved less than an hour ago." As Joe groaned, the captain continued, "The Klack Agency sold it. They're right on the ball."

Fire in his eyes, Joe hurried back to Klack's. Only the girl clerk was there. The boy demanded to know why passage had not been given to him.

"I get my orders from Mr Klack, not you," she replied sourly, and began to pound a typewriter.

Angry and mystified, Joe returned home. When

Frank heard the disturbing news, he said, "Something queer about it all. I'm beginning to think that somebody doesn't want us to sail on a freighter."

"What'll we do now?" Joe asked. "Mr McClintock will be calling up here——"

"And won't find us." Frank grinned. "We're going out to Chet's. He phoned that he needs our help badly. He's pretty sore at us."

"We *have* neglected him," Joe agreed. "Wonder how much of his forty-five dollars he's earned?"

"He hasn't started his fly-tying business yet."

The Hardys found Chet sitting on the back porch of the Morton farmhouse, surrounded by a vast assortment of tools and equipment for tying flies. He looked important and busy.

"Quite a layout, Chet," Frank said as he sat down on the steps.

"Looks as if you're working real hard," Joe commented with a dash of sarcasm as he sat down. But instantly he jumped up with a yelp and detached a small hook from the seat of his pants.

"Not a bad catch," Chet remarked. "Got a big mouth Hardy bass on the first cast!"

"Okay, you win that time," Joe said sheepishly,

Frank chuckled. "Let us in on the project, Chet."

"Making a trout fly looks simple," Chet said, "but it's really pretty complicated." He had a large book propped up against the leg of a chair which he consulted every few seconds.

Then Chet picked up a size sixteen hook. "I'm trying a Quill Gordon just now. Let's see—black hackle and yellow mallard wings."

"Is this your first fly?" asked Joe.

"I've made two so far. Here's one." Chet reached into a tin box and picked up a weird-looking thing.

The Hardys examined the creation dubiously. It was like no fly they had ever seen before. One wing was bigger than the other, and the hook was completely engulfed in a tangle of furs and feathers.

"Looks scary," Frank remarked. "What is it?"

"Actually," Chet confessed, "I started out to tie a Royal Coachman, but didn't have any peacock feathers, so I decided to turn it into a Grizzly King, but it came out different from what I expected. So I call it a Morton Special."

Frank chuckled, "It's original, at any rate."

"Maybe you could do better." Chet thrust pliers and scissors towards his friend. "There's the instruction book. Go ahead!"

The Hardys recognized the manoeuvre. Whenever Chet began a project, some innocent bystander usually completed it for him. However, they were interested in the fly-tying, so they studied the instructions and settled down to the job.

After Frank and Joe had assembled a large assortment of flies and had lunched at the farm, Joe was eager to go back and work on the freighter reservations.

They said goodbye to their chum and drove to Bayport. At the outskirts of town they noticed a familiar figure getting out of a police car.

"Patrolman Con Riley," Joe said with a grin.

Frank brought the car to a stop. "You're a long way from headquarters," he called out to the officer. "What's up?"

"I'm on a case, Frank."

"What's the trouble? Has somebody been helping himself to an empty house again?"

"Exactly. A burglary."

"Mind if we come with you?"

"Not at all. Maybe you masterminds can solve the case for me!"

The boys joined the policeman as he walked up to a white-and-green frame house.

The name UPDYKE was on the mailbox. Riley rang the doorbell.

Mrs Updyke, middle-aged and pleasant, invited them into the living-room.

"This case isn't as serious as I thought when I telephoned headquarters," she told them. "You see, I've been away from home for the past three weeks—"

"And something was stolen!" Riley put in.

"No. That's just it. Nothing was stolen."

"Now wait a minute," Riley said, astonished. "I'm here to investigate a burglary."

Frank ventured a question. "What actually happened? Did some stranger occupy the house while you were away?"

"Yes. I found that one of the beds had been slept in, and some of the kitchen dishes had been used."

"Indicating," suggested Frank, "that the person was here for several hours at least." To himself he added, "Waiting for the express company to deliver a carton, probably." Aloud he asked, "May I use your phone, Mrs Updyke?"

"Go right ahead."

Frank called the express office. He was not surprised

to hear that a carton had been delivered to the Updyke house, but was amazed to learn that it had arrived there two weeks ago.

"No telling how long this funny business has been going on," he thought.

As he was reporting his findings to the others, Mrs Updyke suddenly gasped and pointed. "The documents—they're gone!"

On the wall the boys saw two rectangular places where the wallpaper was not faded like the rest around it. The missing articles must have hung there.

"Do you think they were stolen?" Frank asked. Instantly he thought of the case his father was working on.

"They were hanging there when I left home," Mrs Updyke replied.

Riley got out his report book and began writing. The woman said that the rare documents were insured, but that she hated to lose them. One was a letter written by Abraham Lincoln, the other a military order issued during the American Revolution.

As soon as the Hardys had heard of the papers, they left the house. Riley stayed on to look for clues.

The boys drove home, eager to report this new development to their father. Fenton Hardy listened attentively.

When they finished, he said, "From what you have told me, I think that the theft of the documents was committed by the person who received the carton. I'd like to talk to Mrs Updyke."

Officer Riley was gone when the boys returned with

their father. The policeman had found nothing of importance.

Fenton Hardy wasted no time. He asked Mrs Updyke a few questions, inspected the living-room, then a kitchen closet where she kept paper and string. On the floor lay a short piece of heavy cord, tied in a knot at one end. Mr Hardy picked it up.

"I figured the thief wouldn't walk out of here with the framed documents unwrapped," the detective said. "They would be too conspicuous. This is the unused part of the cord he tied them with." He turned to his sons. "What does it tell you?" he asked.

"It isn't the sort of knot people usually tie," Joe observed.

"It's a stevedore's knot!" Frank said.

Joe thought they ought to look for the seaman with the scar. "He certainly acted suspiciously. I'll bet if we could lay our hands on him, we'd be able to clear the whole thing up!"

"And maybe find Aunt Gertrude's papers," Frank added. "Say, how about using that copy of Johnson's signature we got from the expressman and see if anyone down at the waterfront recognizes it?"

"Good idea. But drop me off at the house first," Mr Hardy said.

After parking the car near the docks, they made a tour of employment offices and waterfront hotels, keeping their eyes open for the suspect. They showed the signature at each place. But no one recognized either the name or the handwriting.

"If he's a longshoreman he may be working around the freighter that came in about an hour ago," one clerk suggested. "It's the *Annie J* down at Pier Ten."

Frank and Joe hurried to the pier and looked closely at the stevedores working there. The scar-faced man was not among them.

"I wonder if this freighter carries passengers," Joe remarked. "Maybe we can arrange something for Mr McClintock."

Frank turned to one of the men and asked if the *Annie J* had passenger accommodations.

"Dunno," grunted the fellow. "Ask one of the crew. Hey, you up there!" he called out.

High above them, a man came out on the deck.

"These boys want to talk to you!" the stevedore shouted.

The moment the Hardys saw the crewman's face, they recognized the scarred man. *Johnson!*

He knew them instantly, too, wheeled around and disappeared.

"Come on, Frank! The ladder!" Joe scrambled up and over the side of the ship's rail, with Frank at his heels, just in time to see Johnson leap over a stack of hatch covers and race towards the fo'c'sle.

Rushing in pursuit, Frank tripped over a coil of rope and sprawled on the slippery deck. He cried out, and Joe looked around just in time to dodge out of the way of a huge steel hook that came swinging at the end of a boom cable.

Frank scrambled to his feet. "Cut across the other side of the ship," he shouted. "I'll look for him in the fo'c'sle."

Joe, meanwhile, had seen their quarry disappear through a doorway. He yanked it open and stepped inside, finding himself in a narrow passage opening into a galley. Halfway along the passage a flight of steel steps led down to the sleeping quarters.

Joe listened. He thought he heard hurried footsteps below. As he started to descend, someone lunged at him from above and knocked him off balance. He fell forward, crashing heavily to the steel floor at the foot of the stairs.

Joe saw a million bright stars. Then they went out.

· 7 ·

A Weird Tale

THE shock of cold water splashing on Joe's face brought him back to consciousness. He heard a voice saying, "That's enough. He's coming around now."

Joe opened his eyes. Two men crouched beside him. One, a sailor in dungarees and jersey, knelt by a bucket of water. The other, lean, sharp-eyed and grey-haired, was evidently the captain of the ship.

"Feeling better?" the captain asked. "I was getting worried about you, young fellow."

Joe sat up and rubbed his head.

"My brother came on board with me. Have you seen him?" he asked.

"He went chasing some fellow down the ladder a little while ago. What's it all about?"

The men helped him to his feet. "I'm sorry, Captain—"

"Dryden is the name."

"Sorry we made such a commotion, Captain Dryden, but we've been trying to catch that man. When we saw him on deck—"

"Why were you after him?" asked the officer, puzzled. He dismissed the subject of the seaman and helped Joe up the companionway to the deck. At that moment Frank appeared.

"Lost him again," he grumbled. "That guy is as slippery as— Why, Joe, what's the matter?" he asked, noticing how white and unsteady his brother was.

"Somebody shoved me down a stairway."

"Come into my cabin," suggested Captain Dryden. "And explain to me what's going on."

He was cordial and solicitous as he ushered them into his own quarters and the three seated themselves.

"First of all, what are your names?" he asked.

"I'm Frank Hardy, sir, and this is my brother Joe."

The man's friendly smile immediately disappeared. He looked stern and suspicious.

"Hardy!" he cried. "What right do you have barging on to my ship like this?"

The Hardys were dumbfounded at his change in attitude.

"Now get out of here!" he ordered.

"May I ask you a question first, sir?" Frank spoke up.

"Depends on the question."

"Until you heard our names you were very cordial. Now there's a difference. Why?"

The officer had not expected anything so flat and direct. He cleared his throat and grunted. Finally he said:

"Your name does make a difference. I've already been warned against you."

"What?"

"A detective came on board as soon as we docked. Sent by a friend of mine. Told me you boys probably would show up here trying to book passage, but not to let you aboard because you'd only make trouble."

"How did you know he was a detective?" Frank asked, suspicious.

"He showed me his badge. Said he dressed like a seaman because of his work on ships." Captain Dryden studied the boys for a moment. When he continued, some of the coldness was gone from his voice. "Now that I've met you, I wonder if all he told me is true."

"What did he tell you?"

"Before I answer, I'd like to know if you've ever heard of me before."

"No, sir," answered the boys in unison.

The captain started to speak, stopped, then said, "I think you're telling the truth. Well, last year I got into a little mix-up in a foreign port. It wasn't my fault and I thought the whole thing had blown over. This detective told me you had been hired to dig up new evidence and that, if I was wise, I'd keep you off my ship."

"Every word's a lie!" Frank declared angrily. "What did this so-called detective look like?"

Captain Dryden's description fitted the man with the scar.

"He's the fellow we're trying to find," the boy exclaimed. "The one I was chasing! I'm sure he's not a detective!"

"More likely a crook," added Joe. "And I'll bet he's the one who knocked me down the stairs!"

Frank asked, "Do you still feel that you wouldn't want us on board?"

The captain laughed. "Not at all. I'd be glad to have you as passengers, but I doubt that this voyage would interest you. It's just a short run down the coast and back."

"Will you consider us for a longer trip later?"

"If you like. But I won't be taking one for the next three months."

The boys' faces showed their disappointment. They thanked the skipper and rose to leave. As Captain Dryden escorted them to the ship's ladder, he promised to keep a lookout for the bogus detective and said he would let the Hardys know at once if he showed up again.

When they returned home Mrs Hardy reported that Mr McClintock had telephoned several times. "I think he's getting impatient," she remarked.

Frank called him immediately. Mr McClintock was more than impatient. He was angry and querulous.

"How long have I got to wait before you find a ship?" he demanded. "I want action, not promises. If you can't locate one by tomorrow, I'll call the whole thing off!"

Aunt Gertrude, who had been hovering near the telephone, gave Frank a nudge.

"Ask him to dinner," she whispered. "That'll cool him off."

Frank took the cue. The invitation did have a surprisingly soothing effect. After grumbling that he would not come unless they got him back to the hotel by nine o'clock, Mr McClintock accepted.

All smiles, Aunt Gertrude hurried to the kitchen. She was an excellent cook and this time did herself proud. When their guest showed up at six o'clock, he sniffed appreciatively at the tantalizing culinary aroma.

"Nothing like a well-cooked meal," he said.

"I quite agree with you, sir," said a voice from the

doorway, and Chet Morton walked in.

He introduced himself, saying that he had heard Mr McClintock was there and wanted to meet him. Frank and Joe were fearful that Chet might bring up the subject of the bamboo fishing rod and annoy their guest. So Frank said quickly, "How about joining us for dinner, Chet? Aunt Gertrude has something special. I'll show you."

He escorted his buddy to the kitchen and warned him that Mr McClintock was jittery and should not be disturbed by being asked to purchase anything. Chet nodded. A few minutes later the family, except Mr Hardy, who was away, sat down to dinner with their guests.

The irrepressible Chet chattered first about food, then fly fishing. He was so amusing that he won Mr McClintock's admiration in short order.

"I like a boy who relishes his meals," declared McClintock, "and also is interested in fishing."

Chet gave his pals a sidewise glance, and steered the conversation around to the subject of fly tying.

"You tie your own?" Mr McClintock inquired, a gleam of enthusiasm in his eyes.

"Yes, indeed," replied Chet. "I've just gone into the business of making the most beautiful lures imaginable—all by hand—the expert way!"

Frank nearly choked on a forkful of salad.

"Why, this is great," declared Mr McClintock. "I've tied hundreds of flies in my time. Used to be one of my favourite hobbies. You must let me visit your shop."

"Sh-shop?" Chet said weakly, and Frank quickly

got him off the hook by changing the subject.

"Have you done any trout fishing lately, Mr McClintock?"

"No," the man replied, putting down his fork and smiling at Aunt Gertrude. "Lost interest in it. Deep-sea fishing is the thing. More thrills. Better sport. Isn't that right, Miss Hardy?"

"Oh, yes, yes. Of course. Bigger fish, too."

Suddenly their guest looked up, his face wreathed in delight. He snapped his fingers with excitement. "Why, that's it! Why didn't I think of this before? I'll take a deep-sea fishing trip!" He leaned towards Chet. "Do you think you could find a fishing boat and a captain who would take us?"

Frank and Joe were upset. Was he going to give up the freighter idea? Were they going to lose out on the trip? His next remark relieved their minds somewhat.

"Frank and Joe here have been trying to arrange a freighter voyage, but they can't get accommodations. So it may be weeks before we go. In the meantime, we'll do some fishing. I'll pay all expenses. Arrange such a trip for me, Chet."

"I'll try, sir," Chet promised.

During the rest of the dinner he and Mr McClintock discussed deep-sea fishing. Chet talked so knowledgeably about marlin, swordfish, and tuna that Frank and Joe knew he must have read up on the subject very recently.

But after the three boys had taken Mr McClintock to his hotel and were driving home, Chet suddenly gave a deep sigh. "Holy crow, fellows! That was a tough evening on me. What am I going to do?"

"That's easy," Joe said. "Hire the boat and make a giant fly to catch whales!"

Chet groaned. "Listen, you two. You've got to help me!"

"Well, if you insist," Joe said, grinning.

The next morning found the Hardys at a wharf talking to a grizzled veteran of the coast named Captain Andy Harkness. He owned several fishing boats.

"A trip? Sure," he said when they told of Mr McClintock's request. "I'll take you and your man anywhere you like, so long as you don't ask me to cruise off the Barmet Shoals."

"What's wrong with the shoals, Captain?" Frank inquired. "You're not afraid of them, are you?"

"Not me. But I got a terrible fright there last evening and I don't want to go near the place again."

The boys were curious. Captain Harkness was not the sort of man who scared easily. They asked him what had happened.

"Don't know if I ought to tell you," the fisherman grumbled. "Most likely you won't believe a word of it, but it's true just the same."

"Try us," Frank said.

"Some time after sundown," the captain began, "with a high sea running, I got off my course a bit. Suddenly I spotted a freighter to my starboard side. I could see we were on collision course, so I threw the helm over hard, but I couldn't hold my boat against the rough water. I knew I was going to hit the freighter but there wasn't a thing I could do."

"So she rammed you?" asked Joe.

Captain Harkness wagged his head. "She did and she didn't. I'd say I ran right through her! That's the part you won't believe, but it's as true as my name is Andy Harkness. By rights I shouldn't be alive now to tell the tale."

"You ran *through* the freighter?" Frank gasped.

"That's the way it seemed. One minute she's looming up ahead of me big as a mountain, all her lights on, the next minute she's not there at all and my boat is swinging northwards off the shoals."

"And where was the freighter?" Joe queried.

"I tell you, she wasn't in sight!"

"What do you mean?" Frank said. "Where could she have gone?"

The captain gave a convulsive shrug, as if the recollection frightened him. "She was a phantom freighter!" he vowed.

Frank and Joe asked him several other questions, but he stuck to his story.

"Did you see any name on the ship?" asked Frank.

"Yep! Caught a glimpse of her name up on her bow. The *Falcon*, she was called. Never heard of her before. But she's a phantom freighter, that's what she is, boys, a phantom freighter!"

Missing Letters

"GOOD thing Captain Harkness noticed the name of the phantom freighter," said Fenton Hardy after his sons had related the strange story. "It gives us a clue to work on, at any rate."

He went to a bookshelf. Taking down a thick volume, he thumbed through the pages.

"Registry of Shipping," he said, scanning a column. "If there is such a ship as the *Falcon* it should be listed here—and it's not."

"Isn't there a chance this phantom ship is registered under another name?" asked Frank.

"Possibly. But I wonder if the whole thing wasn't a hallucination of Captain Harkness."

As the boys left their father's study they encountered Aunt Gertrude in the hall. She began to fuss again because the carton containing her valuable papers had not been recovered.

"With three detectives in the family, a little thing like this shouldn't be much of a problem!" she said.

"We've been working on it, Aunty," Joe said, though he had to admit their leads had come to little.

"The carton was probably in that barn all the time," Miss Hardy went on. "Did you look through the debris after the fire?"

"There didn't seem to be much point in grubbing through the ruins," Frank said. "Any papers would have been burned to ashes."

"Military medals wouldn't," replied his aunt. "There were a couple of old citations among the papers. I'd like to know what happened to that carton one way or another."

Since Frank and Joe had some spare time while waiting for Captain Harkness to arrange the fishing trip, they drove out to the Phillips house. Permission to search the ruins of the barn was granted, and for the next hour they poked through the debris. Their hands were black with soot and their shirts covered with ashes. Weary of the messy task, they were about to give up the hunt as hopeless when Joe picked up a small object near the front foundation.

"Looks like a penny with a hole in it," he said and cleaned off the metal. He held it to the light. The inscription was now legible. *Good Luck!*

"I've seen medals like this in the stores down at the docks," remarked Frank. "Many sailors wear them."

The boys returned to the house and asked Mrs Phillips if she knew anything about the medal. She said it did not belong to them. Joe then telephoned Aunt Gertrude, who declared that the medal had not been among her possessions.

Frank put the medal in his pocket and the boys left. On the way to town Frank said, "It must belong to our friend with the scar."

"Who else?" Joe agreed.

had nearly reached Bayport when a familiar

overtook them and pulled alongside. Chet Morton was at the wheel. Biff Hooper sat beside him.

"Hi!" Chet said. "We want you to go out in the *Sleuth*. Got something to show you!"

The Hardys followed, wondering what was up. When they reached the boathouse they learned that Chet wanted to go fishing.

"Not just for the sake of fishing, mind you," he explained hastily. "It's a scientific experiment for our trip. I've invented a new fish lure. If it works I'll make a fortune. Look!"

From a cardboard box he produced a weird-looking gadget made of tin and strips of aluminium, barbed with hooks.

"I can't imagine any fish going for that!" said Frank. "What is it?"

"A mechanical herring. Commercial fishermen won't have to use real herring for bait any more. One of my mechanical ones will last a lifetime. I'll sell so many I'll make forty-five dollars like that." He snapped his fingers. "Come on. I'll show you how it works."

They climbed aboard the *Sleuth*. In a few minutes the trim little craft was about a quarter of a mile out in the bay. Chet attached his mechanical herring to a length of heavy line. Then he doused it with a foul-smelling fluid which he poured from a bottle.

Joe sniffed. "Wow! What's that?"

"Herring oil," Chet explained. "A mechanical herring should smell like a herring, shouldn't it?"

"I thought fish couldn't smell," Biff said.

"They do when they've been left out in the

Chet carefully lowered his creation into the water and payed out the line. Frank throttled down the engine to trolling speed, and they cruised out into the bay.

"The whole secret of this lure," Chet explained, "is—Wow! I've got a bite!"

The others stared incredulously at their chum, who began hauling in the line. He finally landed a small sea bass with a shout of triumph.

"I knew it would work," Chet declared proudly. "Just wait until I put that thing on the market. I'll sell thousands. I'll—"

"Look!" Joe said suddenly.

His attention had been attracted by a fast motorboat running offshore. It was speeding crazily from side to side as if out of control. Two men in the craft were fighting violently.

Frank snatched up a pair of binoculars. Through the glasses he saw that the men were apparently battling for possession of a large carton. One of them stumbled back with it in his arms. As the other leaped towards him he raised the box high in the air and hurled it overboard.

His opponent sprang at him, knocking him down with a savage blow to the jaw. Then he lurched to the wheel of the boat and swung the craft away from the rocky shore.

The men and their fight were of no great concern to the Hardys, but the carton was. Could it possibly have some connection with their case? they wondered.

Frank headed for the spot where the cardboard container was bobbing up and down in the water, and Biff and Joe hauled it aboard. The sodden carton, with no marks of identification, was torn open. Frank reached in and pulled out the contents. Nothing but tightly packed wool!

"Why were those two fellows fighting over a box of raw wool?" Biff asked, puzzled.

"That's their business," Chet said impatiently. "Let's go out further and try my herring again."

The Hardys, however, were eager to take the carton home and examine it more carefully for possible clues. They were intrigued by the resemblance to the James Johnson box which had come to their house by mistake. Both young sleuths felt sure there was a link between the two!

In their garage Frank went over every inch of the outside of the box. "Not a mark anywhere," he reported.

Joe, meanwhile, had pulled apart every bit of the compressed wool. There was no trace of anything secreted in the fluffy mass.

"Only one more place to look," said Frank and carefully examined the interior sides of the carton. "Nothing here, either," he added. "Whatever was packed in the wool must have fallen out, either before the guy threw the box into the water or after."

The boys cleaned up the mess and went into the house, where they found that the mystery had taken a new and unexpected turn. Aunt Gertrude, looking grim, met them in the kitchen.

"My papers!" she exclaimed in excitement. "Some of them have turned up. Your father just had a letter about them and wants you to take care of it. Look at this!"

Frank and Joe eagerly read the letter, which was postmarked Hopkinsville, several miles away, and had been mailed the previous day:

Dear Mr Hardy:

I am a dealer in autographs and historical documents. Recently there came into my hands a number of letters in which you may be interested. They were written in 1812 by Admiral Hardy, one of your ancestors. If you would like to consider purchasing these letters, please get in touch with me.

Yours sincerely,
Daniel J. Eaton

The boys gazed at their aunt in astonishment.

"Where did he come across the letters?" Frank asked.

"That's what I'm wondering!" declared Aunt Gertrude. "Because those very letters were in my lost carton. The man has the impudence to try to sell us our own property!"

· 9 ·

Code Numbers

FRANK and Joe lost no time in getting to Hopkinsville and finding Daniel J. Eaton. He was a short, baldish man. His little store was wedged inconspicuously between an establishment featuring antique glass and one selling furniture.

Hopkinsville seemed to have many such places—stores dealing in stamps, coins, and rare books. An ideal spot to dispose of old documents!

"Here are the letters. They're authentic, all right," Mr Eaton told the boys as they examined the Admiral Hardy letters.

"Please tell us where you got these," Frank requested.

"They were sold to me by a Miss Elizabeth Hardy a few days ago," the man replied. "She said the letters had been in her possession for many years."

"Would they be valuable to a museum or to a collector?" Joe asked.

Mr Eaton shook his head. "Not really. To another member of the Hardy family, however, someone such as your father—"

"Then why didn't Miss Elizabeth Hardy offer to sell them to us, instead of you?"

Mr Eaton had a ready reply. "She explained about the family quarrel," he said. "Oh, don't worry, I won't mention it to anyone. Miss Hardy assured me, though, that you would be eager to buy the letters. Said she was in financial difficulties. Otherwise she wouldn't have parted with the letters at all."

"Does this woman live in Hopkinsville?" asked Frank.

"No. Said she came from out of town. Was only passing through. Gave her address as Post·Office Box 499, Trenton, New Jersey. I had never seen her before," replied the dealer. He cocked his head and looked sharply at his inquisitors. "But why all these questions? Doesn't your father want the letters?"

"He wants them, all right, but he doesn't want to buy them. They were stolen from my aunt several days ago."

The boys told Mr Eaton the whole story of the missing carton, said there had been no family quarrel and that the woman was a fraud.

"You mean I'm in possession of stolen property?" Mr Eaton exclaimed.

"I'm afraid you are," Frank replied.

Convinced that the Hardys were telling the truth, Mr Eaton wrapped the letters quickly and handed them across the counter. "I'm no fence for any thieves," he said. "Take the letters. I'll suffer the loss."

"We're sorry, Mr Eaton," Joe said, accepting the package.

"The amount was not large," the dealer went on. "If I got gypped, it's my own fault."

The boys thanked him. Mr Eaton said that while he

had bought only the letters from the phony Miss Hardy, she had offered him a number of old books that also might have been in the carton.

"Perhaps she sold them elsewhere in town," he suggested. "There are some second-hand book-stores and antique shops on the next block. If you look around, you may recover the entire lot."

Before the Hardys left the store they went towards the back to examine some old framed documents hanging on the wall. Mr Eaton said he had bought them in the course of the previous week.

"Quite valuable," he said. "I'm certain they're authentic."

"They *look* authentic," Frank remarked. "We can give you a tip, though, Mr Eaton. Many faked documents are being put on the market. They're so cleverly done it's hard to tell they're frauds. If you're offered any more documents, I'd advise you to study the wording carefully. That's where the forgers who make them slip up."

"Thanks," Mr Eaton said gratefully. He promised to send the Hardys the name and address of anybody offering him documents for sale.

Frank and Joe visited half a dozen other dealers. From a list Aunt Gertrude had supplied, they were able to identify several rare old books, autographed first editions, and a number of historical documents. All had been sold to the dealers within recent days by a grey-haired woman who claimed to belong to the Hardy family.

In every case her description tallied with that of the

fake "Mrs Harrison," though she had used various names.

"She's the one all right," Joe declared. "Now this mystery is beginning to shape up. She and the man with the scar are in cahoots!"

At one shop the young detectives were sure they had uncovered a promising clue. Although the woman had sold Aunt Gertrude's family heirlooms to several dealers under the Trenton address, only one had insisted upon knowing where she was staying in Hopkinsville. To this man she had given her name as Mrs Randall. Address—the Palace Hotel.

The Hardys hastened over to the Palace, a small hotel about a block from the railroad station. There they found the lead was false. No one by that name had stayed there, nor could the clerk recall anyone answering the woman's description.

Joe, thinking perhaps he could recognize her handwriting, looked through the register but found nothing suspicious. "Well," he said, disappointed, as they emerged from the hotel, "that's that."

"Maybe she's still in town," Frank suggested.

Vainly the boys walked up one street and down another. Nowhere did they see the woman nor the man with the triangular scar.

As they were returning to their car, a familiar voice cried out, "Well, look who's here!"

The Hardys turned. Beaming at them, his mouth full of peanuts, stood Chet Morton. With him were two girls—his sister Iola and Callie Shaw.

The Hardys grinned because the girls were their special friends. Frank often dated Callie, while Iola was Joe's favourite.

"Hi!" Callie laughed. "Surprise!"

"I'll say," declared Frank. "What are you doing in Hopkinsville?"

"We followed you," teased dark-haired, dimpled Iola. "Chet called your house. When he heard you were here he decided to come, too."

"I'm glad he did," said Frank, smiling at blonde Callie.

"Just a little business trip, really," Chet remarked grandly. "I've been calling on some of the storekeepers here. Got orders for a dozen mechanical herrings and some Morton Special flies. Now all I have to do is make the herrings, tie the flies, and deliver them.

He produced an order book and thumbed the pages with an air of importance, while Frank and Joe howled with laughter.

"It's not funny!" said Chet. "It means money. Now if you fellows would only help me—"

"Help you?" cried Joe. "How about that deep-sea fishing trip?"

"Guess you're right." Chet became silent.

"Oh," said Callie. "I have something to tell you. It may be important."

"Mighty important, I'd say," observed Chet. "Sounds to me as if you fellows are playing with dynamite. Tell them about it, Callie."

"I will if you'll give me a chance," Callie said impatiently. "While Chet was parking the car, I went over to the railroad station, which was across the street. I had to call a friend of mine. The line was busy. While I was waiting, I heard a man talking in the next booth. I didn't pay any attention until he cried out, 'Those boys are wise guys. They've got to keep out of our business, or their old man won't see 'em for a long time'."

Callie took a deep breath.

"Go on," Frank said.

"Then the man said, 'Yes, I mean the Hardys.' With that he dashed out of the booth and got on a train."

"Did you know him?" Joe asked excitedly.

"No."

"What did he look like? Did he have a triangular scar on his face?"

Callie shook her head. "Not that I noticed."

"Did he mention the name of the person he was talking to?" Frank asked.

"He did at the beginning, but at that time I wasn't paying much attention. I've been trying to remember it. I keep thinking of the word 'duck' but it wasn't that."

"Speaking of ducks," interrupted Chet, "I could go for some food right now. It's been a long time since I've eaten. Let's try that restaurant over there across the street."

While they were waiting for sandwiches and Cokes, Frank and Joe questioned Callie closely about the overheard conversation, but she could recall little more than what she had already told them.

"It's silly of me to forget," she said ruefully. "I know he mentioned the name of the person at the other end of the line."

Chet put on his most sagacious expression. "The best way to remember something," he said, "is to forget about it. I mean, change the subject. Talk about something else. The freighter trip, for instance. You fellows had better book a fourth passage, by the way. Mr McClintock says he wants me to go along. In fact, he insists on it."

"We'll have to find a freighter first," Joe said, "and a big one at that!"

At that moment the waitress brought the food. Chet picked up his sandwich. As he opened his mouth, Callie suddenly cried out, "I know! Duck! Quack! *Klack!* That's the name the man mentioned on the telephone!"

"Good girl, Callie!" Joe praised her, while Chet bit into his sandwich with a smug smile.

"So Klack's mixed up in this whole affair!" Frank said grimly. "I thought so!"

"You know him?" Callie asked.

"We've had the pleasure," Joe muttered, then told about their contact with Klack.

Frank decided to talk to the travel agent as soon as possible. When they had finished their snack, they took Chet and the girls back to the railroad station, where Chet had left his jalopy, and said goodbye.

An hour later the Hardys stepped into Klack's office.

"The boss is out of town," said the girl clerk.

"When do you expect him back?" Frank asked.

She shrugged. "A week, maybe."

"Has he booked passage for us yet?" Joe inquired.

The girl shook her head.

"Pardon me, boys," said a familiar voice. A man stepped up to the desk. "Have you got my tickets, young lady? I telephoned yesterday. Name's Jennings." The man smiled at the Hardys. "You fellows taking a trip, too?"

Mr Jennings taught ancient and modern history at Bayport High. As the girl rifled through a list of reservations he chatted pleasantly with Frank and Joe. He had long planned a freighter voyage down the coast for his summer vacation with his two sons, he said, and now he was ready to leave.

"Here you are, Mr Jennings," said the girl.

The boys gaped in surprise as he paid for the tickets and put them in his wallet.

"I suppose you made your reservations a long time ago, Mr Jennings?" Frank asked politely.

"Oh, no," returned the teacher. "It wasn't until yesterday that I knew I could get away at all. Very quick service."

He strolled out of the office, leaving the Hardys staring after him in astonishment. Annoyed by the agency's unfair treatment, Frank demanded that the girl explain why they were unable to get on a ship while others could.

"You'll have to ask Mr Klack about that," she replied.

The boys left. They were now completely convinced that there was a definite reason for their failure to get freighter passage and that Klack had something to do with it.

"I suggest we try an out-of-town agency," Frank said.

"Right. Southport, for instance?"

"Why not."

The next afternoon they drove to Southport. The

people working in the travel bureau there were a great deal more courteous than at Klack's and the owner more co-operative. While Frank discussed their problem, Joe picked up a copy of the local newspaper lying on the counter and glanced at the shipping notes.

"We haven't anything just now," said the agent pleasantly, "but I'll get in touch with the Neptune Line. It may take half an hour or so."

"Good," said Frank. "We'll come back."

"Hey, have a look at this," Joe said, pointing to an item on the front page. It read:

UNINVITED VISITORS

When Mrs W. C. Armstrong of Rushdale Road returned home yesterday from a vacation trip to Maine, she discovered that someone had broken into her house during her absence and had apparently lived there for several days.

As far as is known, nothing of value was taken, but the police are investigating.

A driver for the Southport Express Agency reports having delivered several cartons addressed to Mrs Armstrong and says they were accepted by a woman claiming to be a relative. The boxes were not found in the house and Mrs Armstrong claims she had not ordered anything delivered.

"Sounds familiar, doesn't it?" said Joe.

"The same old routine. We'd better call on Mrs Armstrong," Frank agreed.

The woman, like Mrs Updyke in Bayport, could tell the boys very little other than what the newspaper had reported. Beds had been slept in and kitchenware used, but nothing was missing.

"The police have searched the house thoroughly," she said, "but my visitors didn't leave any clues. Unless you could call this a clue," she added, taking a ragged slip of paper from the mantel. "I found it in a corner when I was dusting this morning."

Frank and Joe examined the paper. Scribbled on it were some letters and numbers:

$$A23—151—C2—D576—A19395—M14$$

"Can you make anything of that?" she asked.

Frank shook his head. "It could be a motor number, a safe combination, a lot of things. Do you mind if I copy these numbers?"

"Not at all!"

Frank took a notebook from his pocket. "You'd better give this slip to the police," he advised.

"Yes. I'll do that."

After the boys had left the house, Joe said, "I believe it's some kind of code."

"Let's memorize the numbers," suggested Frank. "Just in case we should lose them."

Both Hardys went over them several times until they were sure they would not forget them, then returned to the shipping agency.

"I got in touch with the Neptune Line," the owner told them, "and got reservations for you. One of their freighters, the *Crown of Neptune*, will be leaving in two weeks."

"Can we pick up the tickets now?" Joe asked.

"Not right away. I'll have to wait for confirmation. They'll be ready in a day or so. I suggest that you get passports and vaccination certificates because the ship will be putting in at a couple of Central American ports."

"Fine," said Frank. "We'll take care of that."

They drove back to Bayport, relieved that they would have good news for Mr McClintock at last.

"Two weeks, eh?" he said. "Well, that's not so bad. Meantime, we'll go fishing. Do you know if Chet had any luck yet?"

Frank suppressed a grin. "As far as I've heard he's talked to a Captain Harkness. The skipper told him he'd call him as soon as he has a free day."

"Good."

An hour later Frank, Joe and Chet were at the docks to search again for the man with the scar. Unknown to the boys, a longshoreman followed them at a discreet distance. As they walked towards a truck being unloaded by a stevedore, the man tailing them signalled to the worker.

Instinctively Joe turned around and saw the fellow's strange motions. Then he glanced ahead to see the stevedore throw a carton back on to the truck and duck beneath the chassis.

Joe leaped into action. Racing ahead of the others, he dashed to the truck and looked underneath. The man was crawling out on the other side. Joe ran around just in time to see him dodge through a doorway to a storage shed.

The man with the scar!

"Frank, Chet! I found him!" Joe beckoned furiously.

"He ran in there!"

Joe dashed towards the doorway, but was blocked by two workmen carrying crates on their shoulders. The men moved off slowly, revealing the darkened entrance once again. Joe sprinted forward, just as Frank, running up behind him, shrieked out a warning.

"Joe! Stop!"

Out of the shadowy doorway sped a hand truck. It was loaded but nobody was at the controls!

· 10 ·

Frank in Trouble

"Look out, Joe!" Frank yelled in horror.

Joe dived to safety on the cobbled pavement a split second before the cart whipped by and smashed into the parked truck. Boxes and parcels flew through the air.

Unhurt, Joe scrambled up. He suspected that the fugitive had shoved the hand truck towards him in an attempt to gain time for a getaway in the network of alleys along the waterfront.

He caught sight of the man at a gateway to the dockyard. Then the fugitive vanished from view.

Joe raced in pursuit. As he reached the open gate he got a brief glimpse of the fugitive hurrying up the street, but a moment later he was gone again.

"Probably ducked into one of the stores," Joe concluded. He dashed up the street, not sure which door the man might have entered. Joe looked into two shops, then spoke to a fellow lounging outside a pawnshop.

"I saw a guy run into Fit-Your-Figure-Charlie's a minute ago," the man told him.

Joe rushed to the clothing store. It was apparently deserted. No assistant. No customers. Three clothes dummies were in the front window.

Then Joe heard a groan. He traced it to its source in

an anteroom used for tailoring, and found the shop-keeper unconscious on the floor. In the corner was a sink. Joe grabbed a towel, wet it and put it on the man's forehead. The cold water revived the man and he sat up.

"Guy came in here—slugged me—" he murmured.

"Did he have a scar on his cheek?" Joe asked quickly.

The man nodded. "Knocked me out—don't know where he went."

Both looked up at the sound of footsteps in the door-way. Chet poked his head in. "Hey, what's going on?" he asked.

A hurried explanation followed. Then Joe said, "Help Charlie to the couch in his office, Chet. I'm going to call the police."

He looked around for a telephone but saw none, and stepped outside. Suddenly he paused. From the corner of his eye he had caught a glimpse of the display window. Four dummies stood there, one of them in a raincoat, with a hat pulled low over its head!

Joe remembered that there had been only three dummies in the window before! He stepped back inside, quietly slipped the automatic catch on the lock to the window, and went back to Chet. He drew him aside and told him of his discovery. "I locked him in. He's our prisoner," he whispered.

Chet did not like the idea of being left alone with the fellow. "Where's Frank?" he asked worriedly.

"I don't know. Wasn't he with you?"

"No."

"He must have followed another lead. I'll go find a phone."

Before Chet could object, Joe was out the door. He ran to a drugstore at the corner, called police headquarters, and asked for Con Riley. When he had him on the line, Joe said:

"This is Joe Hardy. Listen, how fast can you make it to Mack Street? Fit-Your-Figure-Charlie's place. I want you to arrest a guy in the window."

"In the window?"

"Live dummy. He slugged Charlie. I think he's the scarred man we're after."

"Be right over, Joe."

The young detective started back to the store. Suddenly he heard a crash. A figure hurtled through the show window and landed on the sidewalk. It was followed by a man in a raincoat.

At the same instant Chet raced from the store and tackled the fugitive. They went down in a heap. The scarred man struggled to escape, but Chet hung on grimly, yelling to Joe.

Joe raced up and helped subdue the suspect. A moment later a police car arrived and Con Riley jumped out. He snapped handcuffs on the man's wrists.

"What's this all about?" the prisoner snarled. "I haven't done anything."

"That's what they all say," replied Riley. "You're coming down to headquarters." Riley then informed the prisoner of his rights.

"Yeah, I understand. When I want a lawyer, I'll tell ya," the man muttered.

Chet and Joe, after making sure that Charlie was all right, climbed into the squad car with Riley and the scowling prisoner. They drove to headquarters. There the man gave his name as John Smith. He denied that he had ever gone under the name of Johnson, that he had ever been to the Phillips house, or that he had received any cartons.

He was booked on a charge of assault and battery. The express-company driver was sent for and identified him as the man who had signed for Aunt Gertrude's missing carton. The suspect said the expressman was crazy, and then maintained a stony silence.

"Any identification on him?" Joe asked Riley after the man had been searched.

"Not a thing," the policeman replied. "Just some figures scribbled on the back of an old envelope. Can't make head or tail of them." Riley produced the evidence. Joe whooped. Scrawled on the paper were letters and numbers:

$$A23—151—C2—D576—A19395—M14$$

"The same as those found at Mrs Armstrong's home!" Joe thought excitedly.

Written beneath the figures was *Falcon*.

"The name of the phantom freighter!" Joe gasped.

"What?" Riley asked.

Joe quickly told him Captain Harkness's story and the officer promised to investigate.

When Joe and Chet arrived at the Hardy home, they expected to find Frank there. But he had not yet come back.

"That's strange," reflected Joe. "I wonder where he went."

For the next few hours the family and Chet anxiously waited for news of Frank. With growing concern, Joe and Chet returned to the waterfront and searched the docks thoroughly, making scores of inquiries. But to no avail!

When they arrived home they found Mrs Hardy, pale and tight-lipped, near the telephone. Her husband was away, and Aunt Gertrude paced up and down nervously. "That man they have locked up in jail—I'll bet he knows what happened," she declared. "If I had my way—"

"But the police have questioned him a dozen times, Aunty," said Joe. "He won't talk."

"What time is it?" asked Mrs Hardy.

"Two o'clock in the morning, Mother," Joe replied. "You'd better go to bed and get some rest."

"I wouldn't be able to sleep. If Frank doesn't show up by seven," said Mrs Hardy, "I'll have to telephone your father."

"No use bothering Fenton until we're sure it's serious," said Aunt Gertrude. "Frank will turn up," she added to calm Mrs Hardy, but to herself she said, "I'm afraid something terrible has happened."

The telephone jangled harshly. Mrs Hardy sprang to her feet, but Joe reached the instrument ahead of her.

"Is this the home of Fenton Hardy?" demanded a rough voice.

"Yes."

"Who is this?"

"Joe Hardy."

"All right, kid. In case you're worrying about your brother, here's a tip. You'll find him on the porch of a summer bungalow about two miles up the Willow River. Better go and get him because he's in no shape to walk home."

"Who's speaking? What bungalow? Is he all right?"

The caller hung up.

"What is it, Joe?" Mrs Hardy asked tensely, and he repeated the conversation.

The message had been ominous, but Joe tried to be cheerful. "Oh, I'm sure Frank's all right. Come on, Chet. We'll take the *Sleuth* and go out there."

"I'm going with you," Aunt Gertrude said brusquely. "Come on, Laura, you too!"

Joe looked up. "Better not. What if it's a trap?"

"A trap? But why?"

"Maybe someone wants to get us all out of the house, for some reason," suggested Joe.

Mrs Hardy was distressed. "Then maybe Frank won't be there at all," she said.

"Oh, I'm sure he is, Mother. But we'd better not take chances. Stay here and call Chief Collig. Tell him where we've gone."

Aunt Gertrude nodded. "Joe is right. Sit down. Laura. We'll guard the house. And if I hear as much as a footstep around here, I'll . . ."

Her voice trailed off.

Mrs Hardy said, "Better phone Biff Hooper and see if he can go with you, so you'll have some help in case you need it."

After calling Biff and asking him to meet them at the boathouse, Joe and Chet hurried off. As they sped through the deserted streets in the Hardys' car, they spoke little. The same question was in their minds,

What had happened to Frank?

If they could have played back a movie of the chase the day before, they might have seen the relief on Frank's face after Joe's narrow escape. Frank's first impulse had been to join his brother and Chet in further pursuit of the fugitive.

But then something caught his attention. On the side of a large box near the truck were the numbers A23—151—C2!

Quickly Frank examined several other boxes. Two of them bore similar numbers. Looking for an address, he found a tag nailed to each carton, marked *Wasp— Dock Three, Bayport*.

Sure that he had stumbled upon an important clue, Frank hunted for the *Wasp*. It was a large motor launch, painted yellow and black, with a small cabin. There were no signs of anyone aboard, so Frank leaped on to the deck near an open hatch. Boxes of cargo were stacked below, to within a few feet of the deck.

Frank lowered himself through the hatch to examine the boxes. They were similar in size and appearance to the cartons on the truck. Numbers were painted on the sides. Some of them were identical with the code found in the Armstrong house.

Suddenly Frank heard voices of men who had come aboard. One said, "We've got to get that stuff to Crowfeet or he'll have a stroke!"

"I'm not going to risk it," argued another. "Too dangerous. We can come back tomorrow."

A minute later a third voice shouted, "Hey, men, we've got to get out of here quick!"

"What's the matter?"

"Hank's been arrested. Bayport's getting too hot for this racket!"

There was a sound of running footsteps on deck. This was followed by a heavy thud and sudden blackness.

The hatch cover had been closed!

Frank heard a bell ring. Engines began to throb, and with a roar the *Wasp* pulled away from the dock.

Frank struggled to keep calm. Should he make his presence known by banging on the hatch cover? No, he decided. He would stay hidden and wait for a chance to escape.

"Wish I had a flashlight," he thought. "I'd like to find out what's in these boxes." Thinking he might identify it by feel, he took out his pocket-knife and tried to open one, but the blade snapped off. "Tough luck!" Frank muttered.

The air in the hold was getting stuffy. Frank climbed on top of the boxes and thrust his hands hard against the hatch cover. It did not budge a fraction.

After an hour had passed, the terror of the unknown began to seize Frank. Perhaps he should shout for help. But even if he tried to attract attention, his shouts would hardly be heard above the roar of the engines. If the launch was bound on a long trip, he might suffocate!

A short time later the speed of the launch diminished. Finally the engines were cut off altogether. The boat swayed from side to side, and shuddered as it bumped against the timbers of a dock.

Frank heard voices. Footsteps thudded overhead. With a rattle and a crash, the hatch cover was hauled away. Frank tried to slip down among the boxes, but was too late. A seaman shouted, "Hey! We've got a stowaway!"

"Take him forward!" rasped another.

Half blinded by the light, Frank was dragged and pushed along the deck towards the cabin.

· 11 ·

Stolen Tickets

UNTIL the first light of dawn edged the horizon, Joe, Chet, and Biff roared back and forth on the river near the two-mile mark. They were discouraged when they found no bungalow. The early-morning mist was heavy, and it was difficult to see the homes off the shoreline of the Willow River.

When the fog lifted, they were more than three miles from the mouth of the river. It was then that they saw a dark figure sprawled on the porch of a deserted cabin.

"Frank!" cried Joe.

He pulled beside a makeshift, half-rotted pier and the boys jumped out. Quickly they ran up the few steps to the porch.

Frank was bound hand and foot and tightly blindfolded, but unharmed. As Joe and Biff cut loose the ropes and whipped off the blindfold, they hurled dozens of questions at him. Frank slowly rubbed his aching arms and legs and got up. "I'm starving," he said. "Do you have any chow with you?"

Joe and Biff stared at each other, but Chet beamed happily. He fished an apple and a package of nuts from his pockets.

"You guys are always kidding me because I never go

anywhere without supplies. See how it comes in handy!" He gave the food to Frank.

"Thanks, Chet."

Frank alternately bit a large chunk of apple and tossed a few nuts into his mouth. When he had finished and thrown the core away, Biff said, "Come on. Let's get out of here. Frank can tell us what happened on the way home."

As the motorboat sped back down the river, Frank related his strange adventure. When he reached the point where he had been hauled out of the *Wasp*'s hold and taken to the cabin, Joe interrupted him excitedly.

"Why, you've practically solved the case. You'll be able to identify those men—"

Frank shook his head. "I didn't really see any of them. I was blinded by the sudden light after being in the dark hold. Then a blindfold was clapped over my eyes. Some guy gave an order; another said 'Shut up!' and after that no one spoke. I couldn't identify them."

"What happened then?" Biff urged.

"They moved me from the *Wasp* to another boat. It cruised around for a while, then I was transferred into a rowboat. One man took me up the river. He was supposed to get rid of me and leave no clues, but I guess he was afraid."

"So he dropped you at the cottage?" Joe put in.

"Right. When he left me, he said, 'Let this be a lesson to you. Mind your own business. Any more snooping and you won't get off so easy!' "

Chet gulped. "If I were you, I think I'd follow his advice!"

"Are you kidding!" Joe protested. "This gives us all

the more reason to nab that gang!"

"By the way," Frank said, "how did you manage to find me?"

"Your unknown saviour called the house."

"Well, that was nice of him. Wish he'd done it a lot sooner," Frank said.

By this time the Hardy boathouse loomed ahead, and soon the *Sleuth* was docked. "Let's go home and get some sleep," Joe suggested. "Then we'd better talk again to that man who's in jail. I'm sure he's the 'Hank' you've heard mentioned, Frank. I'll bet he knows all about the *Wasp* and Crowfeet."

"Good idea," Frank said.

They drove Biff and Chet home. When they finally arrived at the Hardy house, their mother and Aunt Gertrude wept with joy. Aunt Gertrude bustled about the kitchen, preparing breakfast, while Mrs Hardy notified Chief Collig of the boys' safe return.

Then Frank and Joe went to bed and slept soundly until noon. When they came down, their mother said Mr McClintock had telephoned.

"I guess he wants to know if we got reservations," Frank said. "I'll check with the Southport agency and see if the tickets are ready."

But when Frank spoke to the agent he received quite a shock.

"Tickets?" the man said. "You got them already."

"No we didn't," Frank told him.

"That fellow you sent over picked them up early this morning and paid for them."

"We didn't send anyone," said Frank. "Did he give you his name?"

"No."

"Describe him, please."

"In his thirties, I'd say. Dark hair. Since he paid for your fare I had no reason to think he was not on the level!"

Frank groaned. "He stole our tickets!"

The agent was greatly disturbed. "This has never happened to me in all my years in business. It's outrageous. Well, don't worry. When the fellow shows up on the sailing date, we can get an explanation."

"Will you issue us new tickets?" Frank inquired.

"That might not even be necessary. I'll be on the ship personally to look into this."

Frank thanked the agent and put down the telephone. "Somebody is going through all kinds of trouble to prevent us from making this trip," he said to Joe. "Even paid for the fare!"

"You know," Joe reflected, "maybe our friend McClintock is the reason for all this. Somebody might be trying to keep *him* from going!"

"You're right. Let's go talk with him."

Mr McClintock greeted them with a grin. "Sleep mighty late, don't you? When I was a boy I used to get up bright and early—six o'clock sharp. Well, what luck? Don't tell me you haven't got the tickets yet!"

Instead of answering, Frank asked, "Have you any enemies, sir?"

The man peered at him suspiciously. "Enemies? What do you mean?"

"Can you think of anyone who wouldn't want you to go on this trip?"

"You're talking nonsense. Who could stop me?

What's behind all this?"

Frank could not make up his mind whether or not Mr McClintock was evading his question. When he told him about the mysterious stranger who had picked up the freighter tickets at Southport, McClintock was furious.

"They can't do this to me!" he snapped. "I'll take legal action. I'll make them hand over those tickets. Strikes me that you boys have bungled this whole business from the beginning!"

He gazed at them intently. "Or perhaps you don't really want to go on a voyage? Well, I'll handle this myself. I'll get tickets!"

Grabbing the room telephone, he put through a call to Klack's Agency. "Hello!" he barked. "Mr Klack? . . . Oh. This is Thaddeus McClintock at the Bayport Hotel. I want passage for four on the first freighter leaving this port. What's that? Now you listen to me—"

The person at the other end of the wire had to do a good deal of listening. McClintock made the line sizzle. He voiced dire threats as to what would happen to the agency if they did not procure tickets promptly. But apparently his wrathful predictions failed to produce results, because finally he slammed the receiver down and sat back, muttering.

"Fine way to run a business!" he growled. "Said she'd put me on the list. I have a good mind to cancel the whole plan."

"Don't worry, Mr McClintock," Frank said calmly. "We'll get on a freighter. The Southport agent will be there personally to straighten things out."

"Thank goodness for that. Say, what's with our fishing trip, meanwhile?"

"Chet's working on it."

"He's no more successful than you in making arrangements," Mr McClintock grumbled. "Tell him to get going, will you?"

"We will," Frank promised and the boys left. Their next stop was police headquarters. They spoke to Chief Collig, who was an old friend. He listened attentively, then reached for a telephone and asked for information about the *Wasp*. When he turned back to the boys, he frowned.

"The launch doesn't seem to be registered. We'll make some more inquiries. And now, about this man we're holding. You think his name is Hank, and he's part of the gang that wanted to get rid of you, Frank?"

"I'm sure of it. Can I talk to him?"

"Go ahead. If he tells you anything worthwhile, let me know."

A guard showed the boys to the cells. The man with the scar was lying on his bunk, reading a newspaper.

"Hi, Hank," Frank said.

The prisoner looked up, startled. Then his expression became wary. "You made a mistake. My name's not Hank."

"That's what the boys on the *Wasp* call you," Frank replied coolly.

"The *Wasp*?" The prisoner looked alarmed. "I don't know what you're talking about."

"A23—151—C2!" said Frank.

The suspect swung himself off the bunk and strode towards the door of the cell. "Now look," he said thickly. "About those numbers. You can't—"

"What?" Frank asked sharply as the man hesitated.

Hank just stared at the boys. Finally he answered, "I don't know anything about those numbers. Talk to my lawyer."

"Does he represent Crowfeet too?"

The man did not answer. The boys made several attempts to get him to talk, but he stubbornly refused to say another word. Finally they left. But they were sure of two things. He was Hank, and he knew something about the mysterious numbers.

When Frank and Joe reached home they found that their father had returned. He had already been told of Frank's adventure on the *Wasp*, and now listened with interest as his sons reported about their call at headquarters.

"The prisoner recognized the numbers all right," Frank said. "At first we thought he was going to talk, but then he changed his mind."

"Let me see those numbers," his father said.

Joe went to get the copy of the numbers on the crumpled scrap found in Mrs Armstrong's home, and showed it to Mr Hardy.

"So Hank wouldn't talk?" the detective said resolutely. "Well, never mind. I believe I can solve that part of the mystery without his help!"

· 12 ·

Harrowing Experience

ASTONISHED, Frank and Joe, leaned forward to hear their father's explanation of the mysterious numbers.

"It fits in with something I happen to know," Mr Hardy said. "Besides the case concerning the fake documents, I am working on an assignment for a large company manufacturing electric motors."

"Industrial espionage?" Joe asked.

"Not quite. The president engaged me to check on a lot of new motors which bear his trade name but weren't sold by his company. They've turned up in various cities along the coast, but his branch offices and distributors in those places know nothing about them."

"Wouldn't it be an easy matter," Frank said, "to check the serial numbers of the motors that leave the factory against the ones being received at the branches, to be sure of this?" asked Frank.

"That's been done," Mr Hardy replied. "All the invoices match up. If five hundred motors are produced in the factory, those same five hundred reach the branch offices. So I'm inclined to think the extra ones are being assembled elsewhere from stolen parts."

Joe was puzzled. "What have our numbers got to do with it, Dad?"

"They sound like the motor numbers and may have a great deal to do with it. At any rate, I'm going to assign Sam Radley to the Bayport waterfront right away."

Radley had been Mr Hardy's operative for quite some time and both boys had great respect for his abilities.

"Maybe we could give him a hand?" Frank offered.

"Not at this time," his father replied, and with that dropped the subject.

"I did have a little luck on another matter," he said. "Joe, will you ask Aunt Gertrude to come into the library. I think she'll be interested in this."

Mr Hardy unbuckled the straps of a big suitcase he carried on his longer trips. When his sister entered the room, he was removing the wrapping of a flat parcel.

"Recognize this, Gertrude?" he asked, holding up a small picture.

It was an oil painting in an old-fashioned frame, showing the portrait of a stern-looking elderly gentleman with bushy whiskers.

"Great-Grandfather Hardy!" gasped Aunt Gertrude. "That picture was in my lost carton! Where did you find it, Fenton?"

Mr Hardy told how he had come across the picture in Washington while visiting antique shops in search of forged documents. He had recognized the portrait at once, because Great-Grandfather Hardy had stared down at him from over the piano in their home when he was a boy.

"He didn't look very happy in that antique shop."

Mr Hardy smiled. "The proprietor couldn't tell me much about the woman who had sold it to him, along with various odds and ends, about a week ago. She gave her address but it turned out to be a phony one."

Aunt Gertrude said nervously she hoped the rest of the contents of the box would come back to her without much trouble. "There were certain things—" she said dreamily.

Just then the doorbell rang. "I'll get it!" Aunt Gertrude cried and hastened towards the hallway.

Frank glanced at his brother. "Have you noticed how jumpy Aunty has been ever since she lost that box?"

"Every time the phone or the bell rings she practically runs to answer it," Joe agreed. "There's got to be more to it than just those missing letters and papers."

It was obvious that Aunt Gertrude was jittery because she was expecting a message—either a phone call or a letter. Was it in connection with the mystery? the boys wondered.

Aunt Gertrude returned to say that it had been a salesman at the door, and—

The sound of the telephone interrupted her. "I'll take it!" she said quickly. A moment later she called out in a disappointed voice, "It's only Chet!"

When Frank said "Hello," Chet responded in an aggrieved tone, "It's *only* Chet. A fine thing to say about me!"

Frank laughed. "Don't be so touchy. What's up?"

"Tomorrow's the day we go tuna fishing with Captain Harkness."

"Great. We'll be there!"

When the Hardys arrived at the wharf the following morning, Mr McClintock was hopping about like a happy child. Swinging over one of his shoulders were straps holding a binocular case.

"With all my deep-sea fishing, I never went out for tuna," he remarked excitedly. "Wonderful day for it!"

"All aboard!" bellowed Captain Harkness.

A few minutes later the fishing boat pulled away from the wharf and chugged smoothly down the bay. Chet, as leader of the expedition, bustled about importantly. He assigned places to everyone and explained the technique of tuna fishing, about which he had just read.

It was a calm, warm day and the sea was smooth, with only a slight swell. A few miles beyond the mouth of the bay, the captain announced they had reached tuna water. He distributed the rods and herring he had brought along as bait and scattered fresh chum over the side to attract the fish.

Mr McClintock took up his position in a fishing chair, and Chet showed him the proper way to hold the heavy rod. He threw the bait overboard and watched it sink until the end of the leader disappeared from sight. Next, he coiled about fifteen feet of the thirty-nine-thread line on the stern and held it.

"Tuna grow pretty big, don't they?" asked Mr McClintock, becoming a little nervous. "It won't pull me overboard, will it?"

"Could be." Captain Harkness grinned. "But don't worry, we'll rescue you!"

Frank signalled to Chet. "Hey, how come you didn't

bring your own rod? I thought you wanted to sell it."

"I do. But I thought I'd better wait and see how he likes fishing."

"Oh. Well, it sounds like a good idea."

The fishermen had no luck until early afternoon. Suddenly Mr McClintock let out a yelp as there was a tug at the line. Then it started to uncoil fast.

"Strike him!" shouted the captain.

The line straightened out. McClintock yanked the rod sharply upwards. The reel screamed, and he was pulled halfway out of his chair.

"Help me, somebody!" he yelled. "I can't hold on!"

He would have let the rod get away from him, but Chet seized it and held on with all his might. Yard after yard of line unwound as the tuna headed out to sea. Captain Harkness shut off the engines and let the fish tow the boat. Though its heavy weight slowed the big tuna down, Chet had to fight with all his strength to keep from losing the prize.

"He's a monster!" the boy puffed.

The battle went on for a long time. There was nothing the others could do but watch the struggle. Chet was growing tired. Beads of perspiration hung on his forehead.

Suddenly the boat began to swing around. They caught a glimpse of the big dorsal fin and the huge black tail of the tuna above the waters. It was a giant!

"I . . . I can't hold on any longer!" Chet gasped finally. "Take over, somebody!"

Joe and Frank sprang to help him. Joe reached Chet's side first. Slowly the big rod was transferred to him. Gripping it hard, he realized why Chet was so exhausted. It was like trying to hold a runaway horse going at breakneck speed. Nearer and nearer shore the fish raced, showing no signs of getting tired.

"Head him out to sea or we'll go on the rocks!" Harkness roared.

Joe pumped on the line with all his might. It did not work!

"No use!" shouted Captain Harkness. "I'll have to start the engine and pull her away, or we'll pile up on the reef. Chet, get ready to cut that line!"

"Please—not yet!" Joe gritted his teeth. Though the strain was terrific, he was gaining the upper hand. slowly the boat turned. Inch by inch, Joe won the contest. Then, with a rush, the tuna was away again, but this time running for open water.

He took them far out to sea, but after another hour gave up the struggle and at last surfaced. Joe reeled in foot after foot of the line. There was a last wild flurry from the fish as the boat closed in. The launch spun around in a circle.

"Wow!" said Frank as he reached down and grabbed the leader, hanging on while Captain Harkness stood ready to strike with the gaff. The tuna rolled on its side, about forty feet from the boat. Together Joe, Frank, and the captain finally conquered the monstrous fish and swung a rope around its tail.

"Weighs six hundred pounds if he weighs an ounce," Andy Harkness said. "After we tow him back to Bayport, we'll have him put on display."

Mr McClintock rubbed his hands in excitement. He regarded the tuna as his own personal property and seemed to be under the impression that he had caught it himself.

"Most interesting afternoon I've ever had!" he declared.

Captain Harkness swung the wheel over. "We'd better start for home. Won't make as good speed towing six hundred pounds of fish behind us, and I want to get to Bayport before dark."

The fight with the giant tuna had taken more than two hours! The boat had gone only a short distance when suddenly the engine coughed, sputtered, picked up again, gave a convulsive gasp, and went dead. The fishermen stared at each other in consternation.

"Sounds as if we're out of petrol," Frank commented.

"Can't be," the captain said. "I topped her off before the trip."

He tinkered with the engine, spun the flywheel. Then he thrust a rod into the tank. It came out dry. He was dumbfounded.

"No petrol!" he muttered. "I don't understand it. There was enough in that tank to last us all day!"

"You think somebody may have tampered with it, Captain?" Frank asked.

"Could be. I was away from the boat for about half an hour. But I don't know why anybody would be mean enough to do that," he returned slowly. "Most of the men around the fishing wharves know it's a serious thing to run out of fuel when you're in open water!"

Mr McClintock nervously asked what they could do about the situation.

"Radio for help," the skipper replied. He switched on his transmitter. It was dead!

A close examination by the Hardys revealed that it had been sabotaged.

"Now what?" asked Mr McClintock.

"We're not far out," the captain replied. "We'll signal the first ship in sight. Meanwhile, they were drifting slowly towards Barmet Shoals.

"I don't like it!" Andy Harkness said darkly.

They sat and waited, thankful that the sea was calm. Dusk began to settle over the ocean. No one spoke. Chet curled up and went to sleep.

Presently Frank's sharp eyes detected a faint moving glimmer.

"I think I see lights!" he said hopefully.

They stared into the gloom. A distant flicker of red and green. Then across the water they could hear a dull, throbbing sound.

"A freighter. Off our starboard," said Captain Harkness.

The lights bore steadily towards them. The ship's engines became louder and louder. Harkness signalled.

Suddenly the lights vanished. The engines became silent.

"Strange!" muttered Frank.

Captain Harkness gave a hoarse cry. "We're too near Barmet Shoals. I knew it! There's no ship out there at all. It's the phantom freighter!"

· 13 ·

"Mrs Harrison" Again

THE Hardy boys were not superstitious. They had seen
the lights and heard the engines. Somewhere out there in
the darkness there must be a ship. But why had the
lights vanished? Why had she silenced her engines?

Frank flashed an SOS with the captain's light.
Result—negative. They shouted, making as much noise
as they could. But there was no answer.

The night had been cloudy. Now the moon appeared
from behind a ragged cloud bank, casting a pale
radiance across the water. In its weird light they saw a
huge black hulk silhouetted against the sky not a
hundred yards from them!

"Ahoy there!" everyone shouted.

There was no answer from the ship.

"Maybe it's not the same one we heard," Frank
suggested. "This might be a deserted ship."

The moon disappeared again and the big dark shape
was lost to view. The Hardys planned to board the
mysterious ship as soon as dawn came.

That night the marooned fishermen took turns keeping watch and sleeping. Frank and Joe were wide
awake, however, when the first grey light illuminated
the sky. They looked over the starboard side.

The freighter had vanished!

Frank grabbed Mr McClintock's binoculars and raced forward, then aft, gazing through the glasses in all directions. There was no ship of any kind in sight.

"Funny!" he said. "How could she have left without our hearing her? There wasn't a sound all night of engines starting."

Joe, who had followed his brother, was puzzled. "Maybe she got caught in the cross-currents and drifted off?"

Captain Harkness, who had been dozing, came to with a start and cried out, "Cross-current nothing. That was the phantom freighter! Now do you believe me?"

The boys did not answer. During the morning a Coast Guard patrol aircraft spotted the fishing launch. Half an hour later a rescue boat pulled up alongside. Its crew were excited over the size of the big tuna and offered to take the launch in tow.

Captain Harkness indignantly refused, but admitted he could use some petrol. He told the officer about the ghost ship, whose name might be *Falcon*, but his story was received with smiles of incredulity.

"Mr Hardy asked us to search for you," the officer said, "but we didn't bargain on hunting ghost freighters. I'll signal our patrol plane, though, to make a sweep of the area. If there's any derelict or a ship named *Falcon* within three hundred miles, the plane will spot it and report back by radio." With that the rescue boat left.

Soon the fishermen arrived at the Bayport docks. Mr and Mrs Hardy met them, accompanied by Chet Morton's parents. All were vastly relieved to see the adventurers safe. Chet was so ravenous with hunger that he almost forgot to claim credit for helping to capture the tuna. Mr McClintock vowed he never would go fishing again.

"Takes too much energy," he groaned. "I'm going back to the hotel and sleep for a week!"

"There goes your sale! I don't think he'll buy your rod now!" Frank whispered to Chet.

The stout boy nodded glumly. "Just my luck!"

When the Hardys arrived home they were alternately praised and scolded by Aunt Gertrude. "I was pretty sure you'd turn up," she said, "but I was worried. Almost cancelled my trip because of it." She looked at the clock.

"Leaving us, Aunty?" Frank asked in amazement. "Where are you going?"

"To Bridgewater. I'll only be there for the day."

"Who's in Bridgewater?" Joe asked.

"You are inquisitive, aren't you!" Aunt Gertrude said. "If you must know, it's a business trip."

Joe's eyebrows raised in surprise, but he inquired no further.

That afternoon the boys heard the city of Bridgewater mentioned again, but under different circumstances. The manager of the Bayport Express Company telephoned shortly after lunch.

"I've just heard something that might interest you Hardys," he said. "Remember the carton addressed to your aunt that was delivered to the Phillips house?"

"Sure do," replied Frank.

"Well, the same kind of thing occurred in Bridgewater a few days ago. A box was delivered to a certain address. Later it was discovered that the owner was out of town and that the woman who had signed for it had cleared out. Sounds like the same racket."

"You're right!"

"The express company is investigating, of course. I'll let you know if anything further turns up."

"Thank you very much," Frank said.

The news about the incident, close on the heels of Aunt Gertrude's trip there, struck the boys as being more than a coincidence.

"I think we'd better drive down to Bridgewater and do a little checking ourselves," decided Joe.

"Good idea," his brother agreed.

When the boys arrived in the small, pleasant city they called immediately at the express office. The manager told them the details about three strangely claimed shipments.

"I don't think you'll learn much from the people at those addresses," he said. "The police have already checked every angle."

Frank smiled. "We'll try, anyhow."

When they left the office Frank came to a sudden stop. "Now look who's over there!" he said.

In front of a hotel directly across the street two women were in earnest conversation.

"Aunt Gertrude!" exclaimed Joe.

"Recognize the woman with her?"

Joe looked again. Then he gasped. "Why, that's the phony Mrs Harrison!"

Why had their aunt come to Bridgewater to meet this imposter? Confused and puzzled, the boys saw the women enter the doorway of the hotel restaurant.

"We'll have to do a little fancy shadowing if we want to find out what this is all about," said Joe. "Maybe we should call the police. Remember the Bayport police are looking for this woman!"

"Let's wait until she leaves Aunt Gertrude," advised Frank. "If we call the police now, it would put Aunty in an awkward spot, particularly since we don't know what those two are up to."

"I guess you're right. I have a hunch that woman is blackmailing Aunt Gertrude. Maybe she has some of her private letters from the carton and is demanding money for them."

"If Aunty falls for it, she's got a mighty good reason," declared Frank. "I guess that's what she's been so jittery about lately. This imposter must have written or phoned her."

The boys hurried into the hotel and made their way towards the restaurant. From the lobby they could see Aunt Gertrude and "Mrs Harrison" seated at a table near the street door. Frank and Joe slipped in and sat down near a potted palm which shielded them from view. Seeing a waitress bring salads to the others, they ordered sandwiches and soda.

Presently they saw their aunt open her handbag. She surreptitiously took out a purse and handed it across the table. The woman put it into her handbag and brought out a packet of letters which she gave to Miss Hardy.

"Just as I said. Blackmail!" Joe whispered excitedly.

Frank shook his head. "I can't understand it."

Aunt Gertrude got up and walked out of the restaurant to the street. The other woman finished her coffee and prepared to leave.

"Get the house detective," Joe told his brother. "I'll stall her in the meantime."

While Frank hurried into the lobby, Joe got up and walked across to the woman's table, determined to take a bold approach.

"Well, if it isn't Mrs Harrison!" he exclaimed, smiling.

The woman looked up at him coldly. "You've made a mistake. My name isn't Harrison."

"Don't you remember me? I called at your house in Bayport. With the expressman."

The woman's eyes were wary. Hastily she got up. "I was never in Bayport in my life," she snapped.

"Better sit down, Mrs Harrison, or I'll call the police," Joe said.

The threat worked. She turned pale and sat down again. "Really, I don't know what you're talking about," she said.

"I want some information from you. Where do your friends keep the stuff they steal?"

The woman did not answer. Instead, she uttered a low moan, then slumped forward with her head on the table.

"Why, she's fainted!" gasped a waitress, running forward.

Joe got up to help. Then he realized this was just a ruse to get him out of the way. Instantly he ran to the lobby, where he found Frank explaining the situation to a thin eagle-eyed man.

"Our friend has pretended to faint," Joe said

quickly. "Maybe we'd better let her think she's getting away with it."

"Not around this hotel she won't get away with it!" declared the detective.

"I think we can handle it ourselves without the publicity," Joe suggested smoothly. "If you'll see that she's helped out to a taxi, we'll take over."

The detective nodded. He went into the restaurant. In the meantime Frank and Joe walked out to the front entrance and jumped into their car. A few minutes later the false Mrs Harrison was escorted to the street.

"I'm feeling much better now," they heard her say. "If you'll get me a taxi . . . so stupid of me . . . just a weak spell . . . I'll be all right."

"Okay, lady," the house detective said as he hailed a taxi. He helped her in. "Hope you feel better when you get home."

"Thank you."

The taxi pulled away. Frank and Joe followed in their car.

· 14 ·

Spy in the Shadows

THE taxi with the woman suspect gained speed. Frank and Joe followed close behind.

"I wonder where Aunt Gertrude went," Joe said.

"We'll catch up with her later," Frank replied. "Right now I'm very curious as to where *we're* going."

Five minutes later the taxi stopped in front of a rooming house about six blocks from the hotel. The woman got out. She paid the driver and hurried up the steps.

After she had gone inside, Joe stood guard while Frank rushed to a telephone to call police headquarters. When he said a suspect in the express-carton racket had been cornered, he was told that a detective would be sent to the rooming house at once.

"We had a call a few minutes ago that that woman was at a downtown hotel," the officer reported. "She moves fast."

"Aunt Gertrude must have notified him," Frank said to himself.

Within three minutes a squad car pulled up at the kerb and a man from headquarters jumped out. Quickly the boys introduced themselves and said they would like to go into the house with him.

113

"Okay. Come on!" agreed the detective.

The only occupant of the rooming house at the moment, besides the owner, was "Mrs Harrison." They found her packing a trunk in a room that was in a state of disorder. She looked up in alarm.

"Who are you? What do you want from me?"

"Police," said the Bridgewater detective, showing his badge. "Taking a trip, eh? Let's have a look at some of this baggage."

"Not without a warrant, you don't!" the woman snapped.

"Here!" The man pulled a search warrant out of his pocket, then proceeded to check through the belongings in the trunk.

The woman watched him tensely. There was nothing but clothing, shoes, and hair curlers.

Frank and Joe, meanwhile, searched the room. In a corner closet they found a cardboard box. Frank pulled it out. *It was addressed to Miss Gertrude Hardy!*

"Here's the evidence!" Joe exclaimed. He examined the contents. There were old books and pictures, antique jewellery and heirlooms, but no personal letters.

"Why didn't you sell our aunt the whole lot?" Frank asked the woman.

She glared at him. "This box does not belong to me. Someone else must have left it there. I never even saw it!"

"Sorry, lady, but you'll have to come to headquarters," the detective said. He informed her of her constitutional rights, to which she replied with a snort.

Frank and Joe followed the squad car to police

headquarters. The woman was booked on theft and blackmail charges. She refused to say anything, however, and was held for arraignment.

"Aunt Gertrude will make a perfect witness," Joe said.

The Bridgewater police chief thanked the Hardys for their help and gave them permission to take home the top from the carton with Aunt Gertrude's name on it. It was hanging loose and the boys promised to return it if needed as evidence.

"She'll have to claim her property later," he said. "It's a lucky break for us, getting this woman behind bars," he added. "After she's had time to think the matter over, she'll probably start talking. Then we'll nab the rest of the gang."

Frank and Joe left police headquarters and drove around for a while in search of their aunt.

When they could not find her, they went to the railroad station. The train for Bayport had just pulled out.

They hurried home, reaching the house about ten minutes before Miss Hardy arrived in a taxi. When she walked in, both boys were innocently absorbed in the afternoon newspaper. The top from the carton was lying on a living-room table.

"Back already!" exclaimed Joe. "We thought you'd stay a couple of days!"

"I transacted my business sooner than I expected." As Miss Hardy took off her hat her eyes fell on the box top. She blinked, took off her glasses, put them back on again. Then she gasped. "Where did this come from?"

"We found it in Bridgewater," replied Joe.

"You what?" She turned crimson.

"Expressman here gave us a tip," Frank explained. "We rushed over and nabbed a woman in a rooming house."

Aunt Gertrude gave both of them an inquiring look. They knew she was wondering whether they had seen her in Bridgewater. She said nothing, however, and went to her room.

"It isn't often we see Aunty blush." Joe laughed. "She's dying to ask us questions, but she's afraid to. What do you suppose is in those letters? She must have wanted them badly."

"I'll bet they're old love letters." Frank grinned. "Dad said Aunt Gertrude was engaged at one time."

The boys found it difficult to think of their aunt as a romantic person, but Mr Hardy had often told them that his sister was very popular and had had many admirers. Conversation on the topic was interrupted by a telephone call from Mr McClintock.

"I don't like to wait two weeks for that ship," he announced. "Tried to get other reservations this morning. Tell me, what does a man have to do in order to get some? Bring a letter from the president of the Maritime Commission? It's perfectly ridiculous!"

Frank and Joe were secretly amused. Now Mr McClintock was finding out for himself how difficult it was!

"By the way," the man continued, "I went down to the docks and heard someone say there'll be a freighter coming in tomorrow morning. Get down there early and meet the boat!"

"Sure, Mr McClintock. We'll try!" Frank promised.

Following his instructions, they went to the waterfront before breakfast, arriving just as a big freighter pulled slowly up Barmet Bay. As it approached the dock the Hardys were amazed to see that it was the *Hawk*.

"Wonder why she came back so soon," Joe remarked. "She couldn't have sailed very far."

"Bet she's in for repairs," Frank replied. "Say, maybe Captain Sharp will be in a better frame of mind this time and give us passage."

But when the *Hawk* was moored and Captain Sharp came ashore he looked as dour as ever. Nevertheless, the boys decided to speak to him. They walked up, smiling.

"Welcome back, Captain," said Frank. "Carrying any passengers this time?"

Sharp squinted at them. "I'll say you two are persistent," he grunted. "You got my answer last time."

"We hoped you might have changed your mind."

"Well, I haven't. Now stop bothering me!"

Captain Sharp brushed past them, but Joe hung on like a barnacle. "All right, we won't mention it again," the boy said. "But I'd like to ask you something else. Have you ever seen or heard of a ghost ship, a phantom freighter, out beyond Barmet Shoals?"

Captain Sharp turned and glared. "Are you trying to make a fool out of me? Phantom freighter, indeed. Do I look like a.man who believes in fairy tales?"

"There's been talk around here—" Joe began, but the captain interrupted him fiercely.

"That'll be enough of your impudence. Get out of

my way!" He pushed Joe aside and strode down the pier.

The boys decided to eat breakfast at a diner along the waterfront, thinking that perhaps they could pick up some information about a passenger freighter. They had no luck, so they started for home. On the way they found themselves across the street from Klack's Agency. A shabby man sat on a bench in front of the place, idly watching passers-by.

At the same moment Captain Sharp, looking thoroughly preoccupied, hurried into the agency. The Hardys followed and stood listening in the doorway.

Turning to the clerk, Sharp said, "I want to hire another cook. Mine jumped ship."

The girl nibbled at the end of her pencil. "We haven't had many cooks in here looking for jobs lately. If you can wait until Mr Klack comes back—"

"What?" growled the man. "I want to hire a hand and I want him right now!"

The shabby man rose from the bench outside and sidled into the office past the Hardys, to whom Sharp paid not the slightest notice.

"I'm your man, skipper," he said. "How much does the job pay?"

Captain Sharp looked him over from head to foot. He asked a few brusque questions about his experience, a bargain was struck, and the two left.

The girl looked at the boys. "You here again?" she snapped.

Frank, having heard that Klack was away, merely asked if she had booked passage yet for his party. She replied in a bored manner that there were no reservations for them and that they would have to wait until Mr Klack got back.

"Let us know when he returns," said Frank. But from the look on the clerk's face he knew that she would do nothing of the sort.

Reaching home, the boys had a conference with their father and told about the return of the *Hawk*.

"Captain Sharp undoubtedly is in on something crooked," said Fenton Hardy. "We don't have any proof, but his freighter should be watched. As for Klack, I can tell you why he's out of town. The FBI has become interested in his activities."

"You think he's hiding?" Frank asked.

"Yes."

"On the *Hawk*?"

"No. The ship could be searched too easily."

Joe was standing near a front window. He glanced out and saw something that made him step back quickly. "We're being watched," he said.

Mr Hardy and Frank hurried to the window, not close enough to be seen, but enough to look out. Across the street, in the shadows of a tree, a shabby man stood gazing at the Hardy house.

"Why, that's the man Captain Sharp hired as a cook in Klack's office!" exclaimed Frank.

· 15 ·

The Abandoned Farm

"CAPTAIN Sharp definitely has something to hide," Mr Hardy said grimly. "He's afraid we suspect him."

"And that we'd see something if we ever got far enough out of Bayport Harbour!" Joe added.

"Which is precisely what we have to do, and fast. We can't wait a couple of weeks for the *Crown of Neptune* to sail," Frank said. "I have an idea. Suppose Biff Hooper tries to get us tickets at another out-of-town agency."

"Good thought," Mr Hardy agreed. "But you'd better not call him from here. Our phone might be tapped."

"Then how do we contact Biff?" Joe asked.

"Your mother will take care of that," Mr Hardy said with a grin and called in his wife. She readily agreed to the plan that he outlined. On her way shopping she would call Biff from a pay telephone.

"If the spy follows you, we'll tail him," Mr Hardy told her.

But the man remained where he was, seemingly not interested in Mrs Hardy's leaving.

"I must get out of here myself," the detective said. "I almost hope he'll follow me. I may learn something."

He went upstairs. After a while the boys heard shuffling footsteps in the hall. An old man, white-whiskered and bent with age, appeared.

"I won't be long, boys," he croaked, a twinkle in his eye. "Just checking out the *Hawk*. If the guy tails me, don't worry!"

Frank and Joe laughed. Their father's disguise was perfect. The detective went out the back door and made his way towards the corner.

Eagerly the boys watched from the window. Either the suspicions of the man across the street had not been aroused, or else he was posted there to shadow only Frank and Joe. He did not stir.

"I suppose we might as well stay home and wait for Biff's report," Frank said. "Dad's watching the *Hawk* and there's nothing much we can do anyhow."

Their mother returned, saying she had telephoned the message. The boys stayed up late, but there was no call from Biff, and their father had not returned.

Next morning he told them the *Hawk* had sailed ahead of schedule.

"There was nothing suspicious about it," Mr Hardy reported. "I had Sam Radley posted at the docks for the past two days, looking things over. He watched the ship being loaded. Most of the cargo was destined for cities down the coast."

"What did she carry?" Frank inquired.

"Large cans of paint and some machinery."

"Is Sharp's spy still on duty?" asked Joe, walking towards the front window. "He's gone," the boy reported, "but it seems someone else has taken his place!"

A taller, leaner man was strolling back and forth across the street, as if waiting for someone.

The telephone rang. It was Biff Hooper.

"The trip's off," he said to Joe, who had answered.

"Okay," Joe replied. "See you later!"

Biff had spoken in code in case the wire was being tapped. "The trip's off," meant that he was still trying to get reservations.

"I wish we could get rid of that spy," said Joe. "I don't feel like sitting home all day!"

"I've got a plan," Frank said. "If it works, we'll also have a pretty good idea why he was posted here."

The ruse was simple. Joe walked out of the house and headed down the street. The man on the other side eyed him carefully, apparently undecided whether to follow or not. When Joe was halfway down the block, Frank ran out of the house.

"Joe!" he shouted.

His brother turned and looked back.

"Come here a minute!"

Joe ran rapidly towards the house, and Frank called out loudly, "The trip's off."

"The freighter trip?"

"Yes. Mr McClintock says to forget it. He's leaving town."

Joe came up the steps and into the house. From behind the window curtains the boys watched the man across the street. Obviously he had heard enough, for he walked briskly away and disappeared from sight around the corner.

"Pretty good trick!" Joe chuckled. "No doubt he's off to report what he's heard."

"Let's get out of here while he's gone," said Frank. "I'd like to follow up something new. You remember when I was on the *Wasp* I heard a man speak of old Crowfeet? Maybe we can find out who he is."

"How?"

"When we were with Andy Harkness the other day he mentioned an Abel Jedson, an old retired officer. Says this guy knows every ship along this coast and everybody on them. Suppose we ask him about Crowfeet."

"Why not? Come on."

They found Abel Jedson living in a little cottage near the bay, where he could watch the comings and goings of the ships. He was a spry, shrewd man with a stubby grey beard and twinkling blue eyes.

Jedson sat on his porch, listening to the radio. On the window sill nearby was a noisy parrot that squawked, "No boarders wanted!" as the boys came up the walk.

They introduced themselves, and after talking about ships in general, Frank asked, "Have you ever heard any stories about a phantom freighter?"

"Hundreds of them." The old man chuckled. "I've been hearing yarns 'bout ghost ships ever since I was knee-high. All nonsense."

Joe asked if he knew Captain Sharp of the *Hawk*. The old sailor cocked his head to one side and said he had seen the freighter, but knew nothing about her or her captain.

"Ever hear of a man called Crowfeet?" asked Frank.

"Name seems familiar, somehow," mused Jedson.

"I'll try and remember." He twiddled the short-wave dial of the radio and brought forth a barrage of squeals that provoked the parrot to a rasping protest. "Turn it off! Turn it off!" he squawked.

Jedson gave the dial another twist. Suddenly the boys jumped in astonishment. Over short-wave they heard a gruff voice say "A23—151—C2." Then silence.

The numbers printed on the boxes Frank had seen in the hold of the *Wasp*!

"Crowfeet," Captain Jedson muttered, unaware of the excitement the announcement had aroused. "Seems to me it had something to do with a fellow named Harry—that's it—Harry Piper! That's what folks used to call him. Crowfeet!"

"Is he still alive?" Joe asked.

"Don't know. Never heard of him dying, anyway. Captain Harry Piper of the freighter *Falcon*."

"The *Falcon*!" exclaimed Frank.

"That's right. Tell you where you might find out about him. When he was ashore he used to live with his brother John, about ten miles out of town. John had a farm a little ways in from Shore Road."

The Hardys were elated. At last they had unearthed a valuable clue! After thanking Jedson, they got into the car and set off for Shore Road.

The Piper farm was difficult to locate. A man cutting grass in a small country cemetery finally put the boys on the right track. He pointed out an abandoned property next to the cemetery.

"John Piper died last year," he informed them. "No one has lived there since."

Frank and Joe got out of the car and crossed the unkempt fields. The whole place was in a state of neglect. Weeds grew high in the yard. Parts of farm machinery lay rusting by a tumble-down fence. The farmhouse windows were boarded. But the place might hold a clue!

"Let's check out the barn first," Joe suggested.

To their surprise the hayloft was stacked high. On the floor was another immense pile of hay, but upon closer investigation the boys found that it was merely a cover for quantities of cowhides.

"These hides are worth plenty!" Frank exclaimed. "I wonder why they're stored here."

They decided to ask the cemetery caretaker if he knew anything about it, and crossed the fields again to talk to him. The man was amazed to hear about the hides.

"Can't figure it out," he said. "I haven't seen anyone near the farm since John Piper died."

"Did he have a large herd of cattle?"

"Heck, no. Never kept more than one cow."

"Let's go back there," Joe said. "Something funny about this."

Surprisingly a truck had arrived in their absence and was parked in the barnyard.

"We'd better take it easy," advised Frank. "I don't like this."

They approached cautiously, circling to the rear of the barn. Quietly they crept up to the back door and opened it. The place seemed as deserted as before. Then they noticed that the great pile of hay on the floor had been scattered from one end of the place to the other. Stepping inside, they gasped in amazement.

The stacks of hides had disappeared!

· 16 ·

Success and Failure

"WE'D better take a look at that truck," Frank suggested.

But before the Hardys reached the door, there was a sudden murmur of voices and sounds of footsteps above them. They glanced up just as a huge mass of hay came tumbling down directly at them!

Frank, unable to get out of the way, was knocked to the floor by its weight and completely covered. He held his breath to avoid sucking in the dust. When he tried to rise, he was unable to throw off the heavy load.

With a startled cry Joe had leaped back, but too late. Though he was not engulfed by the hay, a hard object struck him on the head. He fell to the floor unconscious!

Frank, struggling to get out, was almost smothered. As he fought his way clear of the hay he heard a man say:

"That'll take care of those kids till we can get the rest of this stuff moved."

"Let's hurry," urged a companion.

Moments later the truck lumbered down the lane. Frank was still clawing at the hay and gasping for air. Stumbling free at last, he saw to his horror that Joe lay motionless. There was a large box beside his head.

It was several minutes before Joe revived. "What hit me?" he gasped.

Frank pointed to the box. When he lifted it, he realized that Joe might have been fatally injured if the box had struck him squarely. He opened it and found an electric motor inside.

"Wow! Maybe we've really hit on something this time," he said. "Dad'll want to see this!"

Fenton Hardy was indeed interested when his sons brought the motor home. He took the number and said he would check with his client. The detective was convinced that the boys had located one of the hiding places for the stolen goods.

"Wool, hides, motors, and documents," Mr Hardy mused as the three discussed the various elements of the mystery. "I believe we're on the track of a big gang who are handling all these things."

"Do you think Crowfeet is the ringleader?" asked Joe.

"Possibly. There certainly seems to be a direct link between him and the abandoned Piper farm. In all likelihood he's a smuggler. He may have lain offshore to send in hides in small boats like the *Wasp*, and received stolen motor parts and who knows what else in return."

"On the *Falcon*?"

"Yes, and I have an idea that Crowfeet was warned and has changed the colour and name of his freighter."

"With some of that paint Captain Sharp had on the *Hawk*!" Frank exclaimed excitedly.

"Then that's why Captain Sharp didn't want us on

board and hired a man to watch our house?" asked Joe.

Mr Hardy shrugged. "It certainly all seems to fit together," he said. "But there are still many questions to be answered. One is, why is a smuggler mixed up with the faking of documents found in various states of our country? Well, your good work has made more work for me." The detective smiled. "I must be going!"

After he left the house, Frank and Joe continued to talk over the aspects of the case, which still puzzled them. What was the strange abandoned ship they had seen? Where had it gone? What of Captain Harkness's story about the phantom freighter named the *Falcon*?

The conference was interrupted by the arrival of Biff Hooper. The tall, pleasant boy brought good news. Beaming, he held up four tickets.

"Reservations!" He grinned. "You sail from Southport day after tomorrow."

The Hardys could hardly believe their ears. After all the difficulties they had experienced it seemed impossible that Biff had succeeded in securing accommodations so quickly.

"You didn't go to that Southport agency again, did you?" asked Frank.

"No. Of course not. After somebody filched your tickets there before, I didn't think they'd trust me. I went to one in Eastport. It so happened that they had some cancellations."

Eagerly Frank and Joe examined the precious tickets which were for one of the freighters of the Neptune Line—the *Father Neptune*.

"The ship docks at Southport tomorrow and it's

sailing for the Caribbean Islands and South America," Biff explained.

"Boy, it sounds great!" Joe said. "Mr McClintock sure will be glad to hear this. I'll give him a ring." He went to the telephone, but Frank stopped him.

"Let's go tell him personally," he suggested. "Then Biff can collect the money his father laid out for the tickets."

The three hurried out of the house, piled into the convertible, and drove to the Bayport Hotel.

"I knew it! I knew it was possible," said Mr McClintock, rubbing his hands in glee when he heard the news. "Thank you, Biff. Thank you."

Mr McClintock kept cash in the hotel safe. He paid Biff, then began talking about all he would have to do to get ready for the trip. The boys left him, broad smiles on their faces. They recalled the time he had suddenly decided to go on the *Hawk* and had given them ten minutes in which to get prepared.

The Hardys' next stop was at the Morton farm. They expected Chet to whoop with joy at hearing the news about the voyage on the *Father Neptune*. But he did nothing of the sort.

"Say, what's the matter with you?" Joe exploded. "Don't you understand? Here's your ticket for South America, all expenses paid!"

"Sorry, fellows," Chet groaned. "I can't go with you. I'll be here in Bayport, working my head off, tying flies and trying to sell them, while you're out on the ocean having a wonderful time."

"What happened?" Frank asked.

Chet explained that he was not allowed to go on the

trip unless he first paid back every cent of the money he had borrowed to buy the forty-five-dollar rod.

"I thought you were going to try to sell it," said Joe.

Chet hung his head. "Before I had a chance, I ran over the rod with the car in the garage and ruined it."

Frank and Joe looked at each other. "I don't believe it!" Frank said.

"It's true," Chet concluded drearily. "You'll have to go without me. Take Biff in my place."

Biff, however, showed no enthusiasm. Neither did the Hardys. The zest had gone out of the trip. It would not be the same without Chet.

Suddenly Frank brightened. "I've got it!" he declared. "I know what we'll do!"

· 17 ·

Danger at the Carnival

"STEP up—step up, ladies and gentlemen! The greatest bargain at the carnival! For a few cents, ninety-nine to be exact, less than a dollar, you can buy the lures that catch the biggest fish! Step up—step up! Fine hand-made flies!"

Chet Morton, red-faced and beaming, paused for breath. Then he blew a loud blast on a bugle. When the startled people attending the Southport carnival jumped and looked his way, he held aloft a handful of bright-coloured flies and went into his speech again.

"You risk no money. You merely make an investment in a fish dinner. Every fly guaranteed to pay for itself in fresh trout!"

Few of those who stopped to look had any intention of buying flies. But they drifted closer, attracted by the boy's sales talk. Many of them laughingly parted with a dollar bill. Several men said, "Keep the change, son!"

Chet was having the time of his life! He had started his venture with the help of the Hardys, his sister Iola, and Callie Shaw. They had stayed up most of the night tying flies, and in the morning had obtained permission for Chet to sell them. By noontime the girls had decorated a handsome stand at the carnival.

After Chet was well launched, they left him and went to see the *Father Neptune*. Her skipper, Captain Gramwell, was a slender, white-haired man who welcomed the boys and girls courteously when they came on board the freighter.

It was a big, modern vessel with passenger cabins that were large and airy. The ship itself was spotlessly clean and the crew moved about briskly and efficiently.

"I'm a little upset," Captain Gramwell confided to the Hardys. "Not more than an hour after we reached port I lost one of my best men. He took sick while he was in town and had to be taken to the hospital. Fortunately the man who brought the message had good references and experience, so I hired him to replace Sanderson."

When the Hardys and their friends had left the ship, Frank said, "Something doesn't ring true about that story."

"But Captain Gramwell appears perfectly honest," Callie remarked.

"Of course. But doesn't it seem strange that some sort of misfortune struck his ship the moment we got passage? Captain Gramwell's men have been with him a long time. Now a stranger suddenly joins the crew. Couldn't he be one of the gang working against us?"

"You mean he put the seaman in the hospital on purpose?" Joe gasped.

"There's one way of checking up," Frank decided. "We can go to the hospital and inquire about Sanderson."

They left the girls at the carnival and went to Southport's only hospital. The receptionist shook her head. "There's no one here by that name," she said. "There must be a mistake."

The boys were now convinced that their suspicions were well founded. They decided to go back to the ship and meet the new seaman. On the way out, Frank saw a figure dash from the shrubbery on the hospital grounds and run across the lawn. Frank gave no indication that he had seen anything suspicious. When they reached the gates at the entrance to the driveway, he grabbed Joe by the arm.

"Quick! In here!"

Swiftly they darted into the shelter of the big stone pillars.

"What's up?" asked Joe.

"I saw someone run across the lawn after we came down the steps. We're being shadowed."

A moment later they heard rapid footsteps on the concrete walk. Frank and Joe edged further out of sight behind the pillar. A man walked past. He looked puzzled, glanced from left to right, up the street, back over his shoulder. Then he quickened his pace, hurried on, and disappeared around the next corner.

"Looks familiar," Joe commented. "Where have we seen him before?"

"He's the first spy who was watching our house."

"That settles it. Let's go back and warn Captain Gramwell."

They wondered how the skipper would receive the news. Possibly he might even ask them to cancel their passage! The captain's attitude, however, was just what the boys had hoped it would be.

"I'll have no monkey business on my ship!" he declared angrily. "I'd like nothing better than to get my hands on those crooks. As soon as that new man shows up, I'll find out what's what!"

They did not have long to wait. Within a quarter of an hour a tall, lean sailor came up the gangplank with a duffel bag over his shoulder.

"There he is!" snapped the captain. He turned to the mate. "Go ashore and get me a policeman. If Sanderson has met with foul play, it will be very bad for this character."

When the new hand climbed over the side, the Hardys blinked in amazement.

"Why, he's the second spy!" Joe exclaimed.

Seeing the boys he wheeled around quickly and would have taken to his heels, but Captain Gramwell leaped forward and blocked his escape.

"Now then!" snapped Gramwell. "What happened to Sanderson? Where is he, and what did you do to him?"

"I told you, Captain. He's in the hospital."

"That's a lie. Now speak up, and fast!"

The man turned sullen. "You've got nothing on me. I'm not talking."

The suspect would not admit anything and was taken to headquarters. There he was searched, but only a wad of compressed wool was found in his pockets.

The Hardys persuaded the sergeant to keep questioning the man, who had arrogantly refused the assistance of a lawyer. Finally he shrugged and said:

"Sanderson isn't sick. You'll find him in an old house outside of town. Tied up. I took him there because I wanted to ship on board the *Father Neptune*. He's not hurt."

The sailor, who gave his name as Joe Flint, could not post bail, so he was jailed. Captain Gramwell and the Hardys went with the police in a squad car to the house Flint had indicated. There, in a tumble-down, empty dwelling, they found Sanderson. He was tied hand and foot, exhausted by his hopeless struggle, but otherwise unharmed.

Captain Gramwell had him taken back to the ship and ordered that he be given the best of care. Sanderson tried to express his gratitude to the Hardys for the part they had played in his rescue.

"You'll have plenty of chances to thank them in the next few weeks," the captain told him. "They're sailing with us."

"And that reminds me." Frank laughed. "We left a friend at the carnival, trying to raise money so he can go along. We'd better drive back there and see how he made out, Joe."

The carnival was in full swing when they returned to the grounds. They found Chet in front of his stand, brandishing a fistful of flies.

"How's business?" Frank asked.

"Sold nearly everything. Another five dollars and I'm in. Take over for me, will you? I want to get something to eat!"

As Chet headed for a lunch stand, Frank took his place at the booth and Joe cut loose with a lusty bellow of "Step up—step up, ladies and gentlemen." In another half hour Frank handed out the last Grizzly King. Chet's goal had been reached!

They hurried to tell him the good news and arrived at the lunch stand, to find that Chet had eaten only two hamburgers. He had just given another order for two more. Frank and Joe, who were very hungry themselves, joined him.

As Joe chomped on his burger, he swivelled his stool and watched the archery range across the way. People were shooting arrows at a large target which rotated slowly.

A man in dungarees and a seaman's sweater bought a quiver of arrows. He fitted one and pulled the bowstring. Suddenly he whirled around and let it fly.

Joe froze when he saw the whizzing arrow. The man had aimed straight at Frank!

· 18 ·

"You'll Never Come Back!"

THERE was no time for Joe to push his brother out of the way.

"Down, Frank!" he yelled.

Frank ducked. The arrow zipped over him, embedding itself in the wall behind the lunch stand.

Joe jumped up, dashed towards the assailant, and grabbed him by the shoulder. "What do you mean shooting at my brother?" he demanded.

The man looked embarrassed. "I—I couldn't help it. Someone jostled me and I lost my balance. Sorry about that!" With that he escaped Joe's grip and quickly disappeared in the crowd.

Frank and Joe followed the suspect as he hurried through the busy carnival grounds. They had to do some fancy footwork to catch up with him. Near the entrance they saw him arguing with another man. As the Hardy's moved closer, keeping well out of sight, they heard him say angrily:

"A bargain's a bargain. I want my money!"

"You didn't do the job!"

"Even if I didn't get that kid for you, I tried. Now pay me or I'll shoot something at you!"

As the young detectives reached the pair they

138

recognized the other man instantly. He was the spy who had trailed them at the hospital.

"Get the police!" Frank whispered to Joe.

Joe nodded and left. Meanwhile, Frank listened to the men, who continued their argument and nearly got into a fight. The wrangle ended with the quick arrival of two policemen, who collared the suspects and put them under arrest on charges of attempted assault preferred by the Hardys.

"Looks as if we're rounding up the gang one by one," said the Southport chief of police to the boys at headquarters. "You've done a fine piece of work."

Just then a sergeant walked into the chief's office with a message that the Bridgewater police had been trying to locate the Hardys.

"What's up?" Frank asked.

"They merely said a prisoner had decided to talk if you would come."

"It must be that woman who blackmailed Aunt Gertrude," said Frank. "Let's go."

The boys got into their car and stopped at the carnival to pick up Chet, who had just closed his stand.

"We're driving to Bridgewater," Frank announced. "Want to come?"

"Maybe I'd better," Chet said. "That way I won't spend my money!"

When the Hardys arrived at headquarters in Bridgewater, the chief told them that it was indeed the prisoner "Mrs Harrison" who had asked for them. She was brought out in charge of a policewoman. To the disappointment of everyone, however, she did not speak about the case.

"The reason I wanted to talk to these boys is just to ask them a question," she said. Then she turned to the Hardys. "Are you going on a freighter trip?"

"Why?" asked Joe. "And how did you know about it?"

"Never mind how I know," she replied. "Are you going?"

"Maybe."

"Don't!" the woman said earnestly. "I mean it. I'm warning you. Don't go!"

"Why not?" asked Chet, looking uneasy.

"Because you'll never come back alive!" said the woman.

She got up and nodded curtly to her guard, indicating that the interview was at an end.

All the way home the boys pondered the reason for her warning. Chet was visibly nervous.

"I wonder if I should take time off from my work," he said, "and go on that trip. Now that the fly-tying business is on its feet, maybe I'd be foolish to quit."

"Your licence was only good for one day," Frank teased. "Admit it, you're plain scared!"

"Me scared? Of course not. You don't think I took that woman seriously! But say, maybe it wouldn't be a bad idea to have Biff go along, too, if we could get an extra ticket."

"You'll have to ask Mr McClintock."

The Hardys, though they did not show it, were deeply concerned about the woman's warning.

"Let's phone the jail and find out if she's had any

visitors, mail, or other messages," Frank suggested.

Their inquiry brought no results. The woman had seen no one and received no mail.

"I suppose her warning was given for spite," Frank concluded.

The young detectives continued their preparation for the trip and were ready to sail the next day. In the meantime Mr Hardy had gone over a code with the boys until they had memorized it.

"If you come across any information about the smugglers, send your message in this code to Sam Radley at this address in Boston. I'll be in and out, so you might not always get me," he told them.

At the Southport pier there was laughter and excitement mixed with a certain amount of tenseness. Mr and Mrs Hardy, Aunt Gertrude, the Mortons, and the Hoopers had gathered to watch the departure of the *Father Neptune*.

Mr McClintock, who had invited Biff, was already aboard and kept running around, getting in the crew's way until finally the first mate suggested firmly that he go to his stateroom.

Presently a whistle blew. The boys hurried up the gangplank. Minutes later tugs pushed the freighter away from the dock. Out in the deep water the tugs cast off, and the ship's engines began to throb steadily. Soon she swung off through the gap at the mouth of Southport Bay and headed out to sea.

After unpacking some of their luggage the Hardys went on deck and found Chet and Biff already there. Chet was wondering when and where dinner would be served.

"This sea air gives me an appetite," he remarked.

Just then they saw Mr McClintock hurrying down the deck. He had a slip of paper in his hand and looked intensely worried.

"I've just had a shock. A terrible shock!" he gasped. "Look what I found in my cabin. Pinned to my pillow!"

He held out the note with shaking hands. Frank took it and read the typed message:

This is your last warning. Go ashore before it's too late!

Frank tried to calm the man by suggesting that the note was a practical joke, but he was worried just the same. Later on, in the privacy of their stateroom, he discussed the warning with Joe.

"Either one of the gang slipped on board for a few moments before we sailed, or has shipped with us," he said.

"But Captain Gramwell says every member of the crew has been with him for a long time. Do you suppose we have a stowaway?"

Frank shrugged. "Let's speak to the captain."

With the captain they made a search of the ship, but found no one in hiding.

The *Father Neptune* headed southwards on her course down the coast, and everything went smoothly. The passengers retired early. Their bunks were so comfortable, and the salty air so fresh and tangy that they slept well and forgot all fears they had about trouble on the ship.

The next morning the Hardys roamed about the freighter, keeping their eyes open for a stowaway, and at the same time learning something of the duties of the crew. They visited the sailors' quarters in the fo'c'sle, then went down into the engine room.

It was as compact and efficient as a navy vessel. On the way up they met Sparks. The radioman had a message for the Hardys. "Can't make head or tail of it." He laughed. "It must be in code."

While Chet and Biff were talking with Mr McClintock on deck, Frank and Joe took the message to their cabin. It was from their father. They deciphered the code without difficulty. The message read:

Important to locate the phantom freighter. Smuggling gang eludes authorities by clever disguises. Suspect Klack is aboard. Use every precaution. Dad.

The Hardys decided to tell Captain Gramwell about it right away. As they reached the bridge Frank suddenly stopped short. "Hey, Joe, this ship is listing badly to starboard!"

Just then an excited seaman darted past them, yelling:

"Captain! The cargo's shifting! We're going over!"

· 19 ·

Crowfeet

CAPTAIN Gramwell was barking orders over the loud-speaker:

"All hands report to the hold to move shifting cargo! Delay may mean disaster!"

Frank and Joe dashed below deck. Chet and Biff followed them. In the hold, men were heaving crates of cargo to the portside, their bodies glistening with sweat. They worked frantically. The heavy thud of boxes was the only sound, except for an occasional sharp command.

The boys were directed to a post where the men had formed a double line and were swiftly passing cargo from one to another. Together the Hardys caught the bulky cases as they came, and then tossed them on, their arms working like machines in high gear.

On, on, on came the cases in rapid-fire succession. Minutes passed, and each box felt heavier than the one before. The boy's backs ached, their hands stung. Their breathing turned into short painful gasps for air, and streams of perspiration rolled down their faces. But to let up for even a fraction of a second would throw off the whole operation.

Finally, after what seemed an eternity but was only a

few minutes, there was a perceptible movement underfoot. Slowly, reluctantly, the ship rolled to an even keel.

"We've righted her!" shouted the officer in charge.

The boys went up on deck. As they were discussing what had happened, Captain Gramwell came over to thank them for helping out. Then he shook his head, muttering grimly:

"I can't understand it. How could that cargo have been loaded so badly—whoever was in charge is going to hear about it!"

Frank and Joe looked at each other. The same thought had been running through their minds. Then Frank spoke up. "I thought we should tell you this, sir. We think that it was done deliberately, because we shipped with you."

Joe told him about the woman's warning. "You'll never come back alive!"

The captain was incredulous. "Why, it's fantastic that anyone would go to such lengths!"

Next, the boys informed him of the note left for Mr McClintock, and finally showed him the decoded radio message from Mr Hardy.

"Well!" sputtered the captain. "One thing I can do is to have Sparks contact every ship in this area. If there is an unknown freighter around, we'll do a little investigating!"

That afternoon he called the boys to his cabin, and told them he had received a report on all vessels known to be within a three-hundred-mile radius, and had then established radio contact with each.

"Only one ship reports seeing something strange,"

he said. "There's an unidentified freighter that seems to be drifting. No signs of life, no response to signals."

The Hardys were sure that it was the smugglers' ship. Captain Gramwell promptly set his course towards the position indicated.

"Should sight her before dark," he said.

His estimation was correct. The sun had just touched the horizon when the report came from the crow's nest.

"Freighter on the starboard bow!"

They soon glimpsed the dark silhouette of a ship. Captain Gramwell gazed at the vessel through his binoculars.

"Just as reported—no sign of life. It may be a derelict."

The *Father Neptune* drew steadily closer. "It's called the *Black Gull*," the captain said. "I think I saw a man run across the deck just now and dive behind the fo'c'sle cabin."

Captain Gramwell ordered flag signals run up, in case the *Black Gull*'s radio was out of commission. But there was no answer. Instead, there came a puff of smoke from the *Black Gull*'s stack and the freighter began to move!

"She's on the run!" Captain Gramwell exclaimed as he rang for full speed ahead. "That's no derelict!"

"Will she get away from us?" Frank asked apprehensively.

The captain laughed. "That hulk! No boat of that type can outrun mine."

But to his surprise and fury, the *Black Gull* not only remained out or reach but gradually widened the gap. The captain snatched up the intercom telephone.

"What's the matter down there?" he demanded. "I called for full speed and we're not overtaking that ship!"

"I can't understand it, sir," returned the chief engineer. "We register top speed."

It was growing dark now. Captain Gramwell. puzzled by the inability of his vessel to catch up to the clumsy-looking *Black Gull*, ordered a searchlight trained on the fleeing vessel.

Frank. meanwhile, slipped down to the radio room and coded out a message to Sam Radley in Boston.

Believe phantom freighter Black Gull has been sighted but cannot overtake.

He gave its approximate position and handed the message to the radio operator, then hurried back on deck.

By this time the *Black Gull* had escaped the probing searchlight and vanished into the night. Captain Gramwell stalked the bridge in a rage. His pride was hurt.

"There's not a freighter in these waters faster than my ship!" he insisted. "I can't understand it."

Frank went back to the radio room. As he walked in, there was a faint burst of signals from the set. Sparks shrugged. "Just numbers," he commented. Frank, who was familiar with the international code, cried out in surprise.

The signals spelled out the familiar numbers A23—151—C2!

"That's the smugglers' code!" Frank told himself. "Not the motor numbers at all!"

A few minutes later the signal was repeated. "The smugglers must feel certain," Frank thought, "that their code won't be recognized." Again came the numbers.

"Can you get a fix on that radio?" Frank asked.

"I'll try," Sparks replied. By contacting another ship and using triangulation he was able to pinpoint a fix on the chart. Soon Captain Gramwell had set a new course, and the *Father Neptune* steamed swiftly through the night.

The Hardys went up on the bridge and stood beside the captain. Finally he gave an order. The searchlight blazed out across the water. Frank and Joe uttered whoops of excitement. The dark mass of the *Black Gull* lay clearly revealed in the light, not a quarter mile away.

But the freighter was no longer in motion. It lay apparently deserted and adrift, just as they had first discovered it.

"Maybe the crew abandoned the ship when they realized we were chasing them," Joe suggested.

"I'll send a boat over to make sure," said Captain Gramwell.

"Let me go, sir," Sparks requested quickly.

"And may we join him?" asked Frank and Joe.

Mr McClintock, who had appeared with Chet and Biff, spoke up. "You two watch your step," he advised. "I feel responsible for your safety."

"Don't worry," Biff said. "They can take care of themselves."

The captain consented to their rowing over. "But don't go aboard unless you're sure no one's there," he ordered. "Just circle the *Black Gull*, and if you hear voices or any sounds of life, come right back. We'll keep the searchlight trained on the ship. You stay out of range of the light so you won't be a target."

Soon the Hardys and Sparks were rowing across the dark waters. Gradually they came closer to the black freighter, lying silent and mysterious in the night. There was not a sound except the steady splash of waves against the steel hull.

To keep out of range of the *Father Neptune*'s searchlight, the three rowed around to the far side of the ship. As they went on slowly in the inky darkness, Joe pulled a flashlight from his pocket and switched it on. It revealed a ship's·ladder dangling over the side of the freighter.

"I guess you were right, Joe," whispered Sparks. "The crew got frightened and took to the boats."

"That would be a stupid move," Frank said. "There's no place to go."

He feared the inviting ladder might be a trap, but they had to take the risk. Joe grabbed it and climbed up. Frank followed, and Sparks came next, after securing the small boat to the lowest rung of the ladder.

Once on deck, they peered cautiously around in the gloom, keeping out of the rays of the searchlight.

"Not a soul aboard," muttered Sparks. "Yessir, they thought they were going to be caught, so—"

The words died in his throat. From out of the shadows sprang a dozen men. The Hardys and Sparks were bowled over like tenpins, and despite a violent struggle, were seized. Then a sardonic voice said:

·   "Didn't know when to stay out of trouble, eh? So

now you're in old Crowfeet's hands! Take 'em below, men!"

They were roughly hauled down a companionway to a cabin. It was brightly lighted, but the portholes were covered with blackout curtains. Here the three faced their captors, who were a villainous-looking lot. The chief was a huge, black-bearded man. He was Crowfeet, leader of the smugglers! He looked his prisoners over, his hairy arms folded.

"Welcome to your new home," he said sarcastically. "Behave yourselves and you'll get along fine!"

"We won't be here long," Frank retorted defiantly. "There'll be help coming by morning."

Crowfeet gave a derisive laugh. "No one can board this ship unless I let him. No vessel and no plane can touch me, as you'll find out. I've got protection!"

Crowfeet turned to his crew. "Order full speed ahead. And if the *Father Neptune* tries to follow, give it the works!"

The smugglers went out. Crowfeet slammed the hatch. The captives heard a clang as a heavy bolt fell into place.

· 20 ·

Captured!

"THIS is a fine predicament!" Joe cried in disgust. He hammered at the door of their prison.

"That won't do any good," Frank said. "We've got to be calm and think this thing out."

"It's like a wild dream," Joe said. "Boy, did we ever fall into that trap!"

"And how!" Sparks added. "We were really suckered into this one!"

"The whole thing just doesn't make sense," Frank said. "That guy Crowfeet is an old coot with just enough brains to sail this tub."

"But a genius he's not. Is that what you mean?" Joe asked.

"Right. There's something deeper behind all this hocus-pocus and I think the answer can be found on this ship."

"What about giving the *Father Neptune* 'the works'? What did Crowfeet mean by that crack?" Joe asked.

"That's what we've got to find out, and mighty soon. Listen. We're under way."

The ship's engines throbbed, and at the same time, a draught of fresh air drifted down upon them from a ventilating duct. Joe glanced up. An idea came to him.

"Frank, that duct might lead to another room. Think I could squeeze through it?"

"Want to try?"

"Sure."

"But don't get stuck, for Pete's sake!"

Joe stood on Frank's shoulders, and using a coin for a screwdriver, removed two screws from the grillework of the ventilator. "It's larger than the size used in houses," he remarked.

"Do you think you can make it, Joe?" Sparks asked.

"I'll have to hold my breath all the way," Joe replied.

He stretched his hands out and put his head and shoulders into the opening. By wriggling, he got himself all the way into the duct. Immediately the flow of cool air stopped.

Joe wormed forward an inch at a time. "If anything goes wrong now," he thought, "I might be trapped in here forever!"

Frank and Sparks, meanwhile, cut off from fresh air, were perspiring in their prison. Frank stood on Sparks's shoulders and whispered into the duct, "Joe, how are you going?"

But his brother could not hear him. Joe snaked along for a while until he had to rest. "Good thing I'm getting some fresh air," he thought. "Thank goodness the ship has some modern conveniences!"

The oxygen renewed his strength and he started on again. The air-conditioning duct seemed to be endless. Another inch. Then another.

Finally he saw a dim light. Or was it only his imagination? His fingers clawed against the metal duct.

Occasionally they touched a seam, giving his nails enough purchase to pull ahead.

Yes, it was some kind of light. Probably seeping through the next grille. Finally Joe reached it. He peered through into a room containing a bunk and a desk.

Joe found two nuts in the grillework. His fingertips throbbed with pain, as little by little he turned the small nuts loose.

With a bang of his fist, the ventilator screen fell outward on to the bunk. Joe struggled to get his hands through the opening. He made it. Now his head. Could he wriggle his shoulders enough to get through? Joe felt as if his back were breaking. He emerged from the air duct like a battered butterfly struggling from a metal cocoon and fell out on to the bunk, semi-conscious.

The room spun around and Joe gasped until full consciousness returned to him. What to do now? First thing was to replace the grille.

He shoved it back in place and inserted the screws lightly. Then, straining to hear any possible noise, he stepped out into the hallway. It was empty.

He moved along catlike, the palms of his hands flat against the metal wall. Presently he came to a door with a warning marked in big red letters: DANGER. STAY OUT.

"Danger to whom?" Joe thought. "Could this possibly be 'the works' that the captain was going to deal out to the *Father Neptune*?" The boy tried the heavy handle and the door opened. He stepped inside.

"Come in, Captain," a voice said.

Joe saw an armed guard, sitting with his back to the door. His gun was pointed at a slender, fine-looking, middle-aged man who was working over a battery of dials and switches. Joe crept up behind the guard, and dealt him a karate chop. He fell off the chair like a log.

The other man looked on in amazement. "Who are you?" he asked.

"Joe Hardy. Quick, lock the door!"

While the man followed his command, Joe briefly explained his presence and asked, "And who are you? What are you doing here?"

The man said he was Professor Elvin Rossiter, a scientist who had developed a unique repelling device. "I can't go into details on how it works," he said. "But it will drive off anything that is propelled by a motor in action."

"So that's it!" Joe said. "This ship is able to repel anybody chasing it!"

The man nodded and went on to explain that he had been captured and forced to set up the machine on the old freighter. "I think Captain Crowfeet's crazy," he concluded.

"Just crazy enough to use your invention for his own nefarious purposes," Joe replied. He added quickly "Is it possible to get a radio message out of here?"

The inventor smiled. "I've been assembling a radio, but haven't had a chance to use it yet." He took the front off a console next to the repeller. "Here it is. Ready for operation."

Joe quickly sent a message to Radley. He explained what had happened and said, "Can you get a speedy sailing yacht? Ship stops anything with motors running." He gave the latitude and longitude, then signed off.

He turned to the professor. "Thanks a million. I'm going back now. Just make believe nothing has happened."

The guard had not yet regained consciousness. Joe propped him alongside the chair and went out the door.

Just then the man came to. "What happened?" he cried.

As Joe crept away he heard Rossiter's reply. "I think you fainted and fell off the chair."

Joe made his way back to their prison. It had a bolt outside that could be pulled upwards. Quickly Joe opened the door and slid in. He manoeuvred the bolt in such a way that it would fall back in place as he shut the door with a slight bang.

"Wow!" Frank said in relief. "I thought something had happened to you!"

"I've had nothing but luck," Joe replied, and told about Rossiter and the message he had been able to send over the radio.

"Great!" Frank exulted.

After their excitement wore off, the three fell asleep, but were awakened a few hours later by Crowfeet. He beckoned them to join him on deck.

"Ha-ha." He chuckled. "I see you've resigned yourselves to your fate and rested calmly."

"What's the use of resisting?" Frank said bitterly. "You're too smart for us!"

"Now you're talking sense, boy. I'm smarter than all the Hardys put together. People call my ship the phantom freighter. Good name for it, eh?"

"You said last night that we'd get along fine if we behaved ourselves," Joe said. "Does that mean you'll let us join up with your crew?"

"I can always use strong hands," growled Crowfeet. "We'll see." He eyed the boys narrowly. "You're pretty clever. Caught on to my code, though in the end that's how I got you here!" He laughed uproariously.

Frank asked if the various parts of the code stood for ships and places. He was told they did. A23 meant the phantom freighter, and in combination with some other number meant a certain ship was to meet the freighter at a designated time and place.

Crowfeet gave orders that they were to be given breakfast, and later they were allowed to go on deck. The boys scanned the ocean but saw no plume of smoke or other sign of a ship.

"Not looking for the *Father Neptune* by any chance, are you?" Crowfeet said sarcastically. "Well, forget it. We're far away from her. She doesn't even know where we are." He added, "Come here. I'll show you something!"

On a staging lowered over the side, two men armed with giant spray guns were directing great clouds of grey paint at the dark hull of the *Black Gull*.

"Sometimes we hardly have time to let one coat dry before we have to change the colour and the name again," Crowfeet bragged. "Get our supplies from launches and never go into port."

"You called your ship the *Falcon* once, didn't you?" asked Frank.

Crowfeet gave the Hardys a superior look. "You

almost found me out while I was using that name, because the motor of that fishing launch went dead. Well, I can't tell you everything! We gotta have some secrets!"

. As time dragged by and no help came, Frank and Joe began to lose hope. Perhaps their message had not been received. Then, suddenly, they noticed a white dot on the horizon. Their hearts leaped wildly. The spot soon enlarged into a snowy canvas. Closer and closer it came, until they recognized a racing sloop under full sail!

Suddenly there was a shout from Crowfeet. "What's that yacht doing out there? I don't like this. Full speed ahead!"

The phantom freighter, its name now the *Red Bird*, rattled and groaned as its speed increased.

"Say, it looks like they're chasing us!" Crowfeet yelled wildly. "My repeller! My repeller! It can't work against a sailing ship!"

He bellowed orders to the engine room. But it was no use. The big sloop soon overtook the *Red Bird*. Over the water blared a crisp command from a bullhorn:

"Stop your engines and lower a ladder! We're boarding you for inspection!"

"Coast Guard!" screamed Crowfeet. He ran towards his cabin for a rifle, but Frank and Joe, hitting him high and low, brought the criminal down with a bone-cracking tackle.

Crowfeet rose to his feet, dazed. A few minutes later an officer came over the side, followed by Fenton Hardy.

After a joyous reunion between the detective and his

sons, Crowfeet learned how he had been outsmarted. Realizing the game was up, he gave his real name, Harry Piper, and threw himself at the mercy of the authorities with a full confession.

Crowfeet had preyed on people in many walks of life. He had even stolen inventions and kidnapped their inventors. Professor Rossiter was not the only prisoner on board. There also was a chemist who had perfected a method of ageing wood and paper. Crowfeet had forced him to counterfeit old documents and letters which were then sold as collectors' items.

"I figured out how to hide the papers in cartons of compressed wool along with ampules of an illegal drug and ship them to the houses of people who were away," Crowfeet boasted. "And if I hadn't had such stupid fools working for me, you'd never have caught me!"

"Like the two who got into a fight in a motor-boat on Barmet Bay and threw a carton overboard?" remarked Joe.

Crowfeet just grunted.

"And you stole electric motors," Frank accused.

The captain admitted that he had. He bragged of how he had outwitted Customs in smuggling thousands of dollars' worth of goods in and out of the country, including the South American cowhides which the boys had discovered in the old barn.

The Hardys also learned that one of the gang had tinkered with the petrol tank and radio on Captain Harkness's boat, fearful they were going to search for the phantom freighter.

"How you kids got passage on the *Father Neptune* I'll never know," growled Crowfeet. "But when I heard you had, I sneaked men aboard the ship to reload the cargo so it would shift."

Klack, too, was found hiding below. The FBI would have one less wanted man to hunt for!

Mr Hardy revealed that the captains of the *Hawk* and the *Wasp* and several others in the gang had been captured already. "James Johnson" had finally confessed his part in the scheme, saying if he had not been greedy and kept Aunt Gertrude's carton, and, with "Mrs Harrison's" help, sold the contents, the Hardys would probably never have caught the gang.

The thief admitted that he had lost his good-luck medal in the Phillips's barn and that his cigarette end might have started the fire.

Because "Mrs Harrison" had warned Frank and Joe about the danger of going on the freighter trip, she would perhaps get a lighter sentence, as well as the man who had telephoned the Hardys, telling them that Frank was on the bungalow porch.

Contact was made with the *Father Neptune*. The worried passengers cheered when they heard the news of the boys' release and the smugglers' capture. As the phantom freighter headed towards it, Professor Rossiter came on deck and joined the Hardys.

"You don't know what this means to me," he said. "I had given up all hope for rescue. Now if I could only find my partner, Thaddeus McClintock, with whom I worked on the repeller before—"

"McClintock!" the boys interrupted in unison.

"Why, yes," Rossiter replied. "Do you know him?"

"He's aboard the *Father Neptune*!" Frank said.

"I'm sure he thought I stole the plans. But now . . ."

When the Hardys witnessed the happy reunion of McClintock and his partner they felt well rewarded for their work.

Mr McClintock beamed. He had been planning to ask Frank and Joe to investigate Rossiter's strange disappearance when they returned from the freighter trip. It was the mystery he had talked about.

"But now that won't be necessary," he said. "How would you like a new car instead? Or something else?"

Frank and Joe stopped him short. "Please, sir," Frank said, "just being able to help round up this gang and have a trip is reward enough."

When the excitement was over, and the *Father Neptune* with McClintock's party was steadily ploughing southwards, the Hardys began to wonder what their next adventure would be. They had no way of knowing then that sinister forces at work in Bayport would involve them in *The Secret of Skull Mountain.*

Suddenly Chet, who had been listening to them, gave a tremendous sigh. "We've had enough mystery for a while," he said. "Let's eat!"

"Nothing better than food, is there, Chet?" Joe quipped.

"There sure is."

"What?" Biff Hooper asked.

"That new car Frank and Joe just turned down!" Chet replied.

Gales of laughter drifted out over the sea.